HAVING THE VAMPIRE'S BABY

CHAOTIC CONCEPTIONS
BOOK ONE

COURTNEY DAVIS

5 PRINCE PUBLISHING
5PRINCEBOOKS.COM

Published by:

5 Prince Publishing and Books, LLC

DBA 5 Prince Publishing

PO Box 865

Arvada, Colorado 80001

This is a work of fiction. Names, characters, places, and incidents are the product of the author's imagination or are used fictitiously. Any resemblance to actual persons, living or dead, events, or locales is entirely coincidental.

Digital ISBN: 978-1-63112-423-5

Print ISBN: 978-1-63112-424-2

Cover design by Marianne Nowicki

Interior design by 5 Prince Publishing

First Edition F09192025

For more information about this title, visit: www.5princebooks.com

To my husband, my biggest supporter.

ACKNOWLEDGMENTS

Thank you to Bernadette for believing in my stories time and again.
Thank you to Cate for helping me to make this story into something that readers will enjoy.

ALSO BY COURTNEY DAVIS

Chaotic Conception Series

Having the Vampire's Baby

The Atlantis Series

The Vampires of Atlantis

Aristotle's Wolves

Descendants of Atlantis

Stand Alone Titles

Butterfly Kisses

The Serpent and the Firefly

A Spider in the Garden

Princess of Prias

Soul Sacrifice

A Shadow Among the Stars

Demons and Tea Leaves

Trusting the Alpha

HAVING THE VAMPIRE'S BABY

PROLOGUE

Felicity Stonecroft was up in the middle of the night, not unusual for her. She was a witch, after all and like most witches, she worked well under the moon's influence. Tonight, she'd awoken knowing she was going to receive a message from the Moon Goddess. So she'd prepared and now sat cross-legged in the backyard of her family home. Her sister was still asleep inside, unaware of the magic Felicity was wrapping herself in. Not that she would care, and Felicity would tell Gina about it over breakfast tea anyway.

Her long blonde hair flowed around her and started to lift slightly with the influx of goddess magic. She wore only her thin white nightgown, and her bare feet dug into the soil as she prepared to embrace whatever the Moon Goddess wanted to provide.

Felicity closed her eyes and let the moon's energy wash over her, she felt a vision coming. It would be a message that would set her on a path to enact the chaos She willed. Felicity let out a cackle at the thought, not only did she thrive in chaos, but she also worshiped the Moon Goddess who was so closely linked to fertility. Fertility was the chosen path Felicity and her sister had dedicated their lives to.

As the vision began to take shape she was unsurprised to find it was set in their fertility clinic. A face she didn't recognize swam into view, and a number she did; *371*. A smile curved her lips because being the one to enact the will of a divine one, especially one bent toward causing chaos, was one of her favorite things about being a witch. And this had all the makings for quite a bit of fun chaos.

CHAPTER ONE

Chastity Martin shivered under the paper-thin gown they'd had her change into—why was the temperature so low? They had half-naked people all over this place, but they couldn't be bothered to turn the air conditioner down? Of course, it didn't help that her legs were spread apart, and her feet were in stirrups while a breeze hit her most private areas.

"Looks like you're ripe and ready," Gina Stonecroft said happily from between Chastity's legs.

Chastity stared up at the ceiling, trying not to second-guess this decision. She was forty, her last serious boyfriend had come and gone over three years ago, and she was desperate to have a child before it was too late. Even if that meant doing it on her own. She was a successful artist, and she didn't need another income to make it feasible, especially considering she worked from home and wouldn't require daily childcare. Most importantly, she wasn't waiting any longer for a man of some kind to walk up to her desperate for a family. She wasn't discounting the need for a male influence on the child, but she had a father still alive and in town who was willing to help her and play that masculine role.

She reminded herself that she hadn't come into this decision without plenty of thought and soul-searching. As with everything in her life outside of her art, she was meticulously planned and researched. That's why she'd come here to the Stonecroft Clinic in Oceanview instead of the humans-only clinic in the nearby city of Larkspring.

This place, run by two witch sisters, was the highest rated clinic in all of California and it had a great track record for artificial insemination, likely because they were able to add a magical push to help things along. The price had been high, but what else was she saving up for if not to make her biggest dream come true. She wanted to be a mother.

"Let's do it then," Chastity said, her voice high with anticipation.

Gina cackled and popped her black-topped head up between Chastity's knees. "I'll go get the specimen you picked, 192 is a great choice, I can feel it."

"Thank you." Chastity watched the short woman walk out of the room and let her knees fall together. She'd agonized for two months over which donor to pick, finally deciding on a young man with hair much like her own dark blonde, and green eyes like hers. She wanted the child to look as much like her as possible. The bio said that the man was into fitness and lived a healthy lifestyle. He enjoyed climbing mountains and biked regularly. She guessed that meant her child would be healthy and active, something she thought would be beneficial. She'd be providing the artistic element to the child and a strong sense of organization.

It would be a perfect combination, and Chastity was ready to love the hell out of the little bundle of joy.

A tall blonde woman entered the room instead of Gina a few minutes later. She wore the uniform of the clinic and Chastity recognized her face from the pamphlets. This was the younger sister, Felicity.

"You are ready to be inseminated, I hear," Felicity said with a bright smile that only did a little to relax Chastity.

"Where's Gina? I've only worked with Gina so far." Chastity didn't do well with unplanned changes, and she pressed her knees together, second-guessing her decision to come here. This didn't feel very professional.

"Oh, she asked me to do this part, I'm the one with the magic push. Just lay back and relax, Chastity. I can already tell that this is going to take well. Some women have to come in for insemination a few times before something grabs hold, but this," she held up a syringe with a very long tube attached, "is going to grab on like nothing you've ever seen."

"Okay." Chastity leaned back with a frown, she didn't like this, but the woman's confidence was comforting, and she definitely didn't want to come back multiple times. She let her knees fall back open. It shouldn't matter that another doctor was performing the insemination, and with the drugs she'd been taking to get ready for this, she knew that she couldn't just reschedule the insemination, she'd have to wait a whole month to come back.

Felicity mumbled some words, and Chastity felt her body relax into a near numb state as the woman started the procedure.

A few minutes later Chastity was getting dressed, it was done. For better or worse she was possibly pregnant and on her way to being a mother, something she'd always dreamed of. She couldn't stop smiling as she left the clinic and drove the short distance to Mooncalled Coffee, owned by her best friend Martha and her husband Glen, both werewolves.

"Chastity!" Martha called out and scrambled around the counter. She had big brown eyes and a bouncing brown bob. She was round with her fifth child and glowing with happiness. She embraced Chastity immediately and sniffed her deeply. "You smell fertile."

"Weird, but thanks," Chastity said with a laugh. "I did it."

"Yay, Glen, make Chastity an herbal tea, and she needs a bran muffin."

"Gross, I want coffee and a doughnut," Chastity said.

Martha rolled her eyes. "You have to think about the baby now, it will want all the healthy stuff, and you should get ahead of the constipation now, trust me."

"It's not a baby yet, it's sperm swimming up my insides in search of an egg."

"That's too much information," Glen grumbled behind the counter.

Martha waved a dismissive hand at Glen and led Chastity out to their favorite table in the sun. "Tell me everything."

"Nothing to tell yet. They put the specimen in and now I just take it easy. I can take a test in a couple of weeks to see if it worked."

"And the guy, you picked the one that looks like you?"

"I did. No one will be able to guess at a father, the baby should be my mini me only maybe a little more athletic," she said with a smile. One of her big fears through this whole process was that she'd end up with a child who looked like someone in town and people would start guessing at its father. She wasn't ashamed of her choice to get artificially inseminated, but it would be annoying to go through the trouble of buying from a sperm bank only to end up with a kid who looked like a guy she could have picked up at the bar for the price of a beer.

"I can't wait to watch you grow and change, Chastity, it's such a fun time."

"It must be, since you've done it over and over," Chastity teased, touching Martha's round belly.

"Well, this might be the last, I'm so tired this time. Forty is not young, as you know."

"Oh, I know," Chastity said. "It's the whole reason I'm doing things this way. No more waiting around for a charming prince. I don't need any kind of man to have a family."

"No, you are much too practical for all that fairytale bullshit," Martha agreed with a grin.

Chastity loved how her friend supported this decision. She'd mentioned it in passing about a year ago to some people she knew in the art community—not really friends, more acquaintances—their reactions had been varying degrees of disbelief. When she'd told Martha, the woman had embraced her and offered to help in any way she could, even volunteering her husband's sperm, which as she'd put it, *was a proven winner*. Chastity wasn't interested in trying out werewolf sperm, but she was glad for the support. She hadn't missed the once-a-month nights out with the artist group she'd stopped going to shortly after that failed conversation.

Glen brought Chastity coffee and a doughnut much to his wife's disappointment, but Chastity thanked him gratefully and bit into the sweet treat. "I couldn't eat this morning; I was so nervous."

Martha gave her a chastising look.

"I'll eat healthy when I know I'm pregnant," Chastity assured her friend.

"If it were a werewolf pregnancy, or any other animal shifter I think, you'd know already because you wouldn't feel so inescapably horny," Martha laughed. "And I hear vampire pregnancies cause an increased blood craving in the days after insemination. Witches … I think they just know with all their magic and shit. You humans are the unlucky ones, they just have to wait for no period or for the throwing up to start."

"Oh fun, I can't wait to lose my breakfast. Hopefully I miss the canvases in my studio as I unload coffee and donut."

"A herbal tea would help with the puking," Martha said smugly.

Chastity rolled her eyes then laughed with her friend. Honestly, she was excited for all the coming changes and signs of motherhood.

"Oh, and we will have babies together who will grow up best friends just like us," Martha squealed.

"I will be glad not to go through it all alone," Chastity said, and she meant it. She relied on Martha for a lot of emotional support, Chastity knew she'd be calling Martha with every worry that came up.

"You are definitely not alone," Martha said, squeezing her hand.

A group of rowdy vampires walked up to the coffee shop. They were young—high school maybe—and all with the telling light skin and reddish-brown eyes. Contrary to mythological thinking, vampires indulged in more than just blood, though they could live on blood alone. They could also go out in the sun, though most avoided it as much as possible since they burned easily and were prone to heat stroke.

"I'd better go help Glen," Martha said, and left Chastity to ruminate over the possibilities of pregnancy while she enjoyed her sugary treat. She supposed she should get used to eating healthier. She'd start tomorrow.

She pulled out her phone and sent a text to her father.

I did it! You could already be a grandpa!!

His reply was immediate.

I already love the little bugger.

Chastity smiled down at the phone. She could do this, because she had the support of the two most important people in her life.

Just then a young couple walked into the café hand in hand. They paused at the doorway and kissed then looked into each other's eyes for a brief moment before continuing in and to the counter.

That was something that she wasn't getting in her life any

time soon, but it was going to be well worth the detour from romance.

Over the next few days Chastity tried to keep herself from thinking about the what ifs and just concentrate on her art. She had a show coming up at the library and she was finishing a few special things for the event. It was supposed to be a literature theme night and so all her paintings were twisted impressions from famous stories. Currently she was working on a Romeo and Juliet where Romeo was the damsel in distress hanging off the balcony he'd been sneaking up, and Juliet was a sorceress spinning a love spell on him. Both of a more mature age than Shakespeare had written, of course.

She loved a good romance, and she hated sad endings. What she really longed for was a love story for herself like the one her parents had. They met in college and fell in love instantly, then moved in together after a month and never separated again. Until her mother had died in his arms of cancer. That was ten years ago, and her father had never really recovered, never dated or showed interest in it. He said he'd had his love; he didn't need another. Sometimes Chastity wished he would find someone else, it didn't have to be another great love, but maybe just someone to spend some time with. Someone to go to dinner with, or to the beach. He wasn't too old for that.

And neither was she, but she had a valid excuse to avoid the dating game, at least for a while. Well, she hoped she did, and after the baby arrived it would be another excuse. What would it be like to date as a mother of a small child without a father? That was going to make for very awkward first date conversations.

She looked down at her flat stomach. "That's okay. It might just be you and me, tiny human, for a long time." She'd taken to talking to the possibility of a child since the insemination. She felt like it encouraged the cells to develop into something viable, letting it know it was wanted and already loved.

CHAPTER TWO

Viktor tried not to hiss at the front desk girl as he demanded to be shown into Felicity's office. Her nametag said *Bobby* and she was just doing her job, he knew that but he'd gotten a phone call that morning informing him that his stored sperm had been used to fertilize a woman. He'd rushed in, hoping to prove they'd made a mistake and it hadn't been his. It couldn't be his because his contract with the clinic specifically stated that the sperm was only to be used with his approval. Because he hadn't made a *donation* to their fertility clinic, he'd deposited into a *storage* account. They hadn't even paid him for it because it wasn't to be used at their discretion.

"Of course. She's expecting you," Bobby said cheerily.

"I'm sure she is," he said under his breath as he followed Bobby through a door and down a hall. He hadn't been here since he'd left the sample and it didn't seem like the place had changed much. The board that held pictures of all the successful fertility treatment babies was more packed, he noted.

"Felicity, Mr. Paulie is here to see you," Bobby announced as she tapped on the office door.

"Send him in," Felicity called back.

Bobby opened the door for him and Viktor hurried past her ready to be told there had been a mistake. Felicity was seated behind a small but messy desk looking much like she had the last time he'd seen her. Long blonde hair in a ponytail and white doctor's coat on. She was smiling at him as if this conversation was going to be just another fertility success story. "Have a seat, Viktor." She motioned to the chair in front of the desk as the door shut behind him.

He sat but he didn't wait to move into why he was here. "What do you mean the sample was used?" Viktor snarled. "It wasn't supposed to be used without my knowledge and consent. I thought that was the whole point of this ridiculous operation. The terms were very specific."

"I understand this is unexpected, but I assure you your sperm was deposited into a very nice woman."

Viktor bared his teeth, it didn't matter what this witch thought was a good match for his sperm, it was supposed to be used only with his explicit permission. This was more than a simple donation to people struggling with infertility. Vampires, like all supernaturals, didn't do things the human way. They didn't just go about their lives knowing children existed around them that were theirs. He *would* know. He would see, and smell, and sense his child and it would be impossible to ignore. This clinic was supposed to help infertile vampire couples with the permission and agreement of the donor who would then help raise the child as a third parent. This flighty witch had just given up his sperm to some random vampire couple!

"Who is it?" Viktor demanded, the names and faces of every vampire in the local coven running through his head. There were more than a few he'd rather take a stake through the heart than be bound to and co-parenting with for the rest of his life.

Felicity looked down at the file she was holding, a smile on her lips that he didn't trust. He should have known better than to come here to this witch-run establishment. Witches couldn't be trusted. It didn't matter that this was supposed to be the best in the area, obviously that ranking system was meaningless.

He had come in the day after a dinner party with his father where the man had tried to set Viktor up with another politician's daughter that he approved of. And when Viktor had refused to go along with it, admittedly in a less than polite manner, his father had spent the rest of the night highlighting his own woes as the father of a deadbeat beach bum son. The man was always looking for the right way to spin a story to suit himself.

The night had left Viktor feeling more angry than usual and had solidified in his mind that he never wanted to give his father the pleasure of being proud of him. Which meant he'd likely never marry just in case he inadvertently picked a bride that his father found acceptable. But that didn't mean he didn't want to have a child someday, one that he could help raise. He knew he could be a tertiary parent to a child, but not a full time one, that way he wouldn't be able to screw the child up too much.

That was the thought that had driven him to the Stonecroft Clinic the next day to deposit his sperm which wasn't supposed to be used unless he approved of the couple it was given to. He figured he would know when the right couple entered his life. Two people with fertility issues, something common in vampires, or a lesbian couple. Either way it would be vampires he knew would raise a child the way he approved. A couple who he could help out and be involved with without being a fully responsible father. It wouldn't derail his life, it would just add a fun and fulfilling piece to it.

"Her name is Chastity Martin," Felicity said brightly, dragging Viktor out of his ruminating.

Viktor frowned. He was certain he didn't know any vampires by that name.

"And the husband?"

Felicity's smile widened as if she were giving him the best news as she informed him that there was no husband.

"What? You let some random vampire woman trap me into being the only father to her child?" This was a nightmare; this was everything he'd been trying to avoid since high school. He had zero interest in being a full-time father. Had zero confidence he could do it well.

She shook her head with a little laugh. "Oh no, don't worry, she has no desire to know who the donor is." She shoved the folder in her desk and stood as if that were the end of the conversation.

Like hell it was. Viktor was going to lose it, he could feel his teeth elongating, ready to tear apart the source of his frustration. Lucky for this little witch, he knew better than to let those thoughts overcome him. He took a few controlled breaths and stood. "You'll be hearing from my lawyer," Viktor said.

"Oh well, there is no need for that. You did sign the *Divine Intervention and Chaos Clause*."

"The what?"

She rolled her eyes. "The *Divine Intervention and Chaos Clause*. We won't be held responsible for the work of any entity seeking to control or cause chaos among our fertility sessions."

Viktor's head was spinning. "You're joking, right?"

"Oh no, it's very serious and holds up in court every time." She beamed at him without an ounce of remorse for what she'd done. "You signed the consent when you donated."

Viktor wanted to smash everything in the room, but he settled for fisting his hands and taking a deep breath. "So, because some trickster god wanted to cause chaos in my life, I am the only father to a child with some random vampire not of my choosing?"

"Something like that," she agreed. "Now, if you'll excuse me, I have another appointment I really must be getting to."

Viktor was too stunned to speak as Felicity hurried from the room. After a few minutes he gathered his wits enough to leave as well. There was a different girl behind the front desk, a cute vampire with dyed blue hair and a pierced eyebrow. He asked her for a copy of the agreement he'd signed. He would read it thoroughly once his brain was a little more settled and he could focus.

If there was any wiggle room to sue, he was going to be in his lawyer's office the next morning.

"Here you are sir." Her nametag said Georgia and he leaned forward, ready for his usual flirtation that ended with him handing her a business card and offering her a free surf lesson. But then she said, "Congratulations."

He scowled at her. What did she know? He hoped she knew that if she broke the confidentiality of this place he'd destroy her. Vampires loved to gossip, and he knew this situation was going to be big news as soon as it got out. "How often does the first insemination work?"

"Oh, it's about fifty percent of the time, but that doesn't account for the intervention of gods, goddesses or other chaos-causing entities," she said in a bored tone as if she repeated herself a hundred times a day.

"This *place* is a chaos-causing entity," he grumbled as he left.

An hour later he was through a cup of coffee, two muffins, and all twenty pages of legal shit he should have read two years ago when he'd gone in to store sperm. He stared down at his signature, scrawled quickly and he remembered, without reading thoroughly. He re-read the pertinent clause now.

All previous permissions become void in the event of intervention by gods, goddesses and other chaos-causing entities including but not limited to: lesser trickster gods and goddesses, demons, and cosmic entities not yet discovered or recognized. The clinic cannot be held responsible for following the orders and/or will of any aforementioned entities.

"All done, honey?" Martha, the pregnant werewolf woman who owned Mooncalled Coffee came up to his table with a smile.

"I suppose so, unless you have a blood bag back there. I think I need something to take the edge off this anxiety," he said with a frown.

"I'll see what we've got. Do you have a preference?"

He shook his head no. She walked inside and he followed, taking his dishes and ready to pay for everything. At the counter his gaze locked onto a flyer with a picture of Little Red Riding Hood, except the girl was a vampire and she'd snuck into the wolf's cave. It was an interesting take on an old story and a beautiful depiction but what really caught his attention was the name.

"What's that?" he asked the teen behind the counter, the couple's oldest son who was cashing him out.

"Art show at the library," he said as if Viktor was an idiot who couldn't read.

"Right, and the artist, her name is Chastity Martin?"

The teen gave an exasperated sigh. "That's what it says, doesn't it?"

"Benjamin," Martha snapped. "Be nice to the customers. Here honey, all we had was type O, so I hope that's alright." Martha set a blood bag on the counter and smacked her son on the back of the head.

"It's great, thanks. Do you have any extra flyers?" he asked, his heart racing.

"Sure thing, honey, here you go. Hope you check out the show, Chastity is amazing."

"I'm sure I will," he mumbled and turned.

"Dude, your blood," Benjamin called.

Viktor turned back and took the bag then left the shop, eyes glued to the flyer. It didn't have her face and he was still trying to place her name to one of the many female vampires in the Oceanview and surrounding area covens. There were three separate covens in the area but they all mingled from time to time. The larger city that butted up to Oceanview was Larkspring and held its own coven, whose members tended to be very sleek, very business professional, where he and the Oceanview coven preferred board shorts. The mountain coven, which resided largely outside the city limits to the east in the foothills, was the least hospitable to outsiders. They were the most wild and usually only came out at night even though the supernaturals had been revealed and welcomed into human society for over fifty years now. He was sure she wasn't part of his coven; he knew them all very well. He pulled out his phone and called one of his friends, Samuel, who happened to be a member of the mountain coven. That seemed like the most likely scenario seeing as Viktor had grown up in the city coven and still knew most of them.

"Yo, Vik, what's up? Are you coming to the bar this week, I want to party."

"I don't know, hey, do you know a vamp named Chastity Martin?"

"No. Kinky name though." Samuel said with a laugh. "Why, should we know her? Want to make her into a sandwich this weekend?"

Viktor rolled his eyes at his friend who refused to be serious, which was usually exactly why he liked the guy, but right now he needed answers. "No, I'm just wondering."

"Well, if you find her and she's hot and fun, let me know. I need a new booty call."

"Sure man, I'll let you know." Annoyance filled Viktor but he wasn't sure why. "Later," he said and hung up.

Viktor made another phone call, this one to his sister, Persia. She had stayed in the city coven, married a man their father approved of, and lived the kind of life befitting the daughter of a politician. She was obviously their father's favorite. Thankfully she'd actually married a guy Viktor could respect and they'd made an adorable little daughter who Viktor adored.

"Hey big bro, what has you calling me finally? It's been at least a month and by the way I'm good, your niece is good too, not that you asked. Also what the fuck, you missed Barry's birthday! My husband is your brother-in-law, you have to at least pretend to care about him. And also—"

"Fuck, can you shut it for a second, take a goddamn breath. I called because I have a question."

"Of course you did, you wouldn't bother calling just to see how I'm doing, would you?" she said with a hint of hurt.

Viktor tightened his grip on the phone, he could practically see her pouting and he wished he'd called her husband instead. He loved his sister, but she was good at guilt-tripping him. "Do you know someone named Chastity Martin?"

"Chastity Martin! She's amazing, such a good artist. My friend, Janessa Cox, you remember her, she brought Chastity in to do a show at the library tonight. Crazy that you mentioned her today. Oh man, she's such a doll, I hear she's just the sweetest thing. Wait, why are you asking about her?"

"No reason, I'll see you soon," Viktor grumbled and hung up on his sister before she could guilt him any more for not being more involved with her life. He just didn't feel like he fit in their lifestyle, actively tried not to, if he were being honest, so he avoided it. Different worlds made him uncomfortable, and it sounded like that's the world Chastity Martin was a part of too.

Given the option, he never would have picked the uptight city coven to raise his child in. But at least his sister seemed to adore the woman, that was one point in her favor. He forgot to confirm she was single, of course asking Persia that would have been like a green flag to involve herself in his love life, not something he wanted.

He had little choice now, he would go to Chastity's show, and he would confront her for taking sperm without the permission of the male. Did she not consider the implications, the complications? Or did she not care? He stiffened as a new thought came to him. Did she not think that she'd have to include him? Did she think that she would be able to keep his child from him? Even worse, was she trying to trap him, *had* she trapped him? He'd be bound to raise this child with her, did she think that meant he'd have to be *with* her? Was this somehow a plan devised by his father? It wasn't impossible to think Johnson Paulie had somehow found out that Viktor had stored sperm. He could have greased a few palms and picked a girl and boom, made his own grandchild just the way he wanted.

The thought brought fire to his veins, how dare they? A familiar loss of control filled him, something he hadn't felt since he'd gotten out from under his father's thumb, and as much as he tried to shake it off, he couldn't. This stranger was the future mother of his child, and he resented her.

With a few hours to spare and knowing he'd never be able to concentrate on anything else, Viktor headed for the ocean. He'd find comfort in the surf and try to tire his mind through his body.

Four hours later Viktor was dragging his board back home. The little surf shop on the beach was his pride, his escape, and usually the place that lifted his spirits. It didn't do much for him today, however. He'd ridden the swells one after another and let the heat of the sun punish his sensitive skin. Now he was just angry, sore, and a little burned.

It was an unusual career for a vampire, surf shop owner and part time surf instructor, but he'd grown up hitting the waves every chance he got, and the ocean called to his heart. It was the first place he'd ever found where his father didn't control everything around him. As for the sun, Viktor slicked his body with the most aggressive, and somewhat experimental, sunscreen out there. He reapplied twice as much as any other species would need to, but he didn't mind. He could even claim to have the slightest tan thanks to years of building up his tolerance. Something that wasn't so uncommon in his coven, but the city and mountain covens found terribly crass. They prided themselves on the palest skin.

He toweled off, rubbing his short blond curls, then locked the shop. He walked around to the back where the staircase to his one-bedroom apartment was. He loved living over his work and even more, he loved living within spitting distance of the ocean. He'd never considered this a great place to raise a child though, and knowing that Chastity had gotten inseminated without being married, possibly not even dating anyone, meant he'd feel an obligation to take the child for long periods of time and doing more than a third of the rearing as he'd planned.

The possibility of having to leave his beachside home over this was just another reason for him to resent her.

He grumbled as he showered and dressed in khaki shorts and a Hawaiian print shirt. Ms. Martin was about to get her dreams blown up at her little art show.

CHAPTER THREE

Chastity was beaming, she knew it, her cheeks hurt from the level of pride and joy she was feeling.

"Oh my god, everyone is going to love this," Janessa squealed. As the head librarian, Janessa was the one who had approved Chastity's art show in their community works space. She was currently stroking Chastity's ego. "You must be so proud of your daughter, Frank."

"Extremely," Frank agreed and squeezed Chastity's hand. "Her mother and I knew she was talented from a very early age. She used to paint masterpieces on her highchair tray with strained peas and applesauce."

Chastity rolled her eyes at the familiar story but Janessa was eating it up. Frank Martin was a tall man with grey hair that was still thick, and glasses perched on his sharp nose. He had been a looker in his youth and still showed the signs of confidence and ease with others. Chastity hadn't inherited that same sociability but tended to be more quiet and passive in groups, much like her mother had been.

Janessa laughed softly as Frank finished his story then turned back to Chastity. "Well, I think you'll sell these easy. If not tonight, then this month while we feature them. I can feel magic in the air ... and that's not just because I'm a witch and spelled my wrinkles away," she cackled.

"Good, I think I'm going to need the cash flow," she said with a grin. She wasn't sure she was pregnant, it was too early to tell obviously, but she *felt* pregnant, as silly as that sounded after just a couple of days. She knew that her tiredness and her slightly engorged breasts could just have been from the hormone injections she was on to help implantation, but it never hurt to hope.

Janessa gave her a quick hug and went to open the doors.

"Are you worried about money, with the—" her father gestured down at her belly.

"No, of course not, but I know that more savings can't hurt and I will likely take a little break from painting once the baby comes. Just padding my nest," she assured him. She knew he worried about her being alone and without a traditional income, but he'd never pressured her to get a real job or to wait for a man who could help support her, and she loved him all the more for it.

"Okay, looks like the crowd has arrived. I'll wander and look impressed so everyone knows that your paintings are special," he whispered and hurried away as a small crowd flowed in.

Janessa started schmoozing and socializing while Chastity took a step back to observe. She wanted to see honest reactions to her art, something she knew she wouldn't get if people knew they were being observed by the artist herself.

It was a mix of people, all ages and species which didn't surprise her for a library event.

As she wandered quietly through the room and listened, she was happy to hear it was mostly complimentary or neutral, and she felt like she was floating as she circulated the space. She stopped near a man, vampire she thought maybe. He had the stiff posture of a vampire, though his skin seemed a bit darker than usual. She couldn't see his eyes from where she stood so she couldn't be certain but there was something telling her this wasn't a human, and he seemed too thin to be a werewolf. Not that he wasn't muscled, she could tell he was in good shape and quite tall, probably close to six feet. That would put him well above her own five and a half feet. He wore a fun and bright flowered shirt that spoke of a personality that was light and adventurous. His golden curls were wild. They seemed to float around his head in a disarray that he hadn't even tried to contain. She let her gaze creep down to his bare legs and smiled at the tattoo on his right calf, it was a sunset over water, a calm scene with bright colors. Down further she saw he wore sandals and there were bits of sand stuck to his feet as if he'd just taken a walk on the beach before coming here.

She was about to walk up to him and stealthily ask what he thought of the painting he was eyeballing. It was a scene from the secret garden but instead of trees and flowers, the children were surrounded by nymphs and fairies disguised as such. Just as she thought to approach, a woman sauntered up to him, a vampire for sure. Chastity could see the telltale glint of red in her dark brown eyes as she flicked her gaze familiarly up and down the man, not bothering a glance for the art.

"Viktor, I'm surprised to see you this deep into the city. Aren't you missing some bodacious waves?" she asked with a raised eyebrow and a pointed look at his feet. She was dressed in a black silk slip dress that hugged her curves perfectly and made her look sophisticated in a way that Chastity had always struggled to achieve.

Chastity had chosen to wear a simple green sundress with low-heeled strappy brown sandals for the event. Her hair was in a braid and as usual, there was paint under her nails. This woman intimidated her.

Viktor didn't spare the woman a glance, just continued to assess the painting. "I'm here to meet the artist, do you know her?"

Chastity perked up at those words, eager to hear how this attractive, at least from behind, male knew of her. Viktor turned to face the woman and Chastity got her first glimpse of his face. It was as handsome as his backside. Strong jaw, broad nose, and full lips. It was a profile she'd like to paint, and her fingers twitched as if she could pick up a brush right then and capture this man's essence on canvas.

"Chastity Martin. Can't you read the sign?" the woman asked with a small scoff. "I didn't realize you beach vamps had let the sun burn through to your brains."

So he was a vampire.

"Helpful as always, Treenly," Viktor drawled.

"Why do you want to meet the artist? Are you going to commission something for your surfboard?" she said derisively.

"As if I would want something this trite and childish on anything of mine," he sneered, waving a hand at the painting in front of them.

Chastity's heart froze and she turned before either vampire noticed her lurking, but she wasn't fast enough to miss the next comment.

"I can only imagine the artist is as reckless and foolish as her work," Viktor added.

Chastity rushed to the bathroom before anyone could see how upset she was. All the while berating herself for breaking down under criticism. It wasn't as if she expected everyone to love everything she did, it was just that she knew how hard she had worked on everything in this show and hearing that the man she'd been ogling thought it was trite and childish was too much under the stress of the whole event.

Or maybe it was hormones, because she usually had a thicker hide than this. Maybe she should have planned better than to have a show just days after artificial insemination and two months of hormone preparation.

She locked herself in a stall and sat down to take deep breaths.

She was debating the likelihood that she could hide out in the bathroom until it was all over when she heard someone else enter the bathroom.

"Chastity, are you alright?" Janessa's voice floated to her, and she knew she wasn't going to be able to stay hidden.

"Oh yeah, just needed to pee, that's all."

"Right, I know that look I saw on your face as you ran in here. Who said something rude? I swear I'll kick them out right now."

Chastity dabbed her eyes with toilet paper and laughed. "Don't do that, everyone deserves to have their own opinions. I'm just a bit emotional tonight."

The old witch sighed empathetically. "I know it's a big night. I'm sorry it's not perfect."

Chastity left the stall and gave Janessa her best smile. "I'm just being silly. I've heard a lot of good things tonight; one negative doesn't matter."

"That's the truth," Janessa agreed but pursed her lips like she wanted to say something else. "Come out when you're ready, I have some people who want to meet you."

"Okay," she said, her voice cracking. What if it was the vamp who hated her stuff? He'd seemed to be looking for her, but why?

Chastity reminded herself that she was a big girl and she was going to take criticism with a smile as she'd done in grad school, because art was subjective and she could only do what she liked and hope at least one other person agreed. She rejoined the party and found Janessa thankfully standing with a werewolf couple who were eager to make her acquaintance.

For the rest of the night, she managed to avoid the vampire who'd upset her, and by the end she'd sold nearly half the paintings and had a couple of leads on possible commission work. She was going to be okay. She touched her belly. Even if she had another precious mouth to feed in nine months, she wouldn't have to resort to getting a regular job any time soon.

. . .

Viktor brushed Treenly off as fast as he could, she'd always irritated him. The fact that their families knew each other, and he'd taken her out on a couple of dates when they were barely out of their parents' houses, added to her irritant level. She knew just enough to get under his skin.

He'd seen her wrinkle her nose at the paintings she'd passed before approaching him so he'd given the easy answer, pretending to hate it far more than he did in reality. It was true that it wasn't his style, much too whimsical, but he knew talent when he saw it and this woman had it. He supposed that was one thing, probably the only one thing in her that he'd appreciate his child inheriting.

The elusive artist was unknown to all the vamps in attendance however, which had him second-guessing his theory that she was a part of the city coven. Perhaps his sister knew her through some other avenue. At his wit's end, he approached Janessa who he'd met through his sister a few times.

"Janessa, good to see you again."

"Viktor, I saw you earlier and was surprised Persia wasn't with you, she usually loves these things."

"Yeah, she mentioned it to me so I thought I'd stop by. Could you point out the artist? I've been trying to figure it out all evening, but she seems to be playing hard to get."

"Oh, Chastity isn't much for the spotlight, that's for sure, and this is her first big show so she's been nervous." Janessa looked around the room and Viktor followed her gaze, skipping over anyone not a vamp. "There's the woman of the hour," Janessa said.

Viktor looked where Janessa was pointing but all he saw was a cute little human and an older gentleman.

"Where?"

"There," Janessa said with a frustrated wave. "The brownish blonde in the green dress."

Viktor froze. "No," he hissed and suddenly she looked up, her green gaze catching on his. He'd noticed her earlier as he'd wandered of course, because she was an attractive woman, but he had dismissed her because she wasn't what he'd been looking for. It couldn't be. "She's human," he spat and not quietly. He knew she'd heard and her face flamed. She looked away then excused herself from the man and headed for the bathrooms.

The man sent a glare his way and Viktor felt a tinge of shame. He probably should have tried to be subtle.

"What the hell do you have against humans, suddenly?" Janessa snapped.

"I have to go," Viktor said and hurried out of the library. He needed air before he made an even bigger scene.

How the hell could this be? It couldn't, could it? Despite the identical physical forms of all four main species, it was rare for them to successfully interbreed.

She likely couldn't become pregnant with his sperm, he realized once he had calmed down from the initial shock, which was a huge relief. But still, she'd been inseminated with his sample and he had to be sure it wasn't one of the rare and unlikely instances of a vampire and human creating a child. With witches and chaos-causing entities involved, though, he wouldn't discount anything.

He didn't go far from the building. Like a storybook vampire, he lurked in the night shadows as the rest of the crowd left the library, and waited for the woman he sought. Finally, the dark blonde-haired human in a green dress walked out clutching a tote bag and talking on a cellphone. He watched her until she got in a VW beetle and drove out of the lot.

"Creeper."

Viktor jumped at the voice and spun around to find Janessa standing behind him with a smirk.

"You got the hots for the artist?"

"No. What do you know about her?" he demanded.

She huffed a laugh. "Yeah, like I would sic a womanizer like you onto that sweet human. Find someone who can handle your crazy, she's too soft."

Janessa left and Viktor sulked on his way back to his own car, a VW van.

A short drive back to the beach shack and a quick google search later brought Viktor to Chastity's website. It was something he should have done right from the start, but he hadn't been thinking clearly all day. He found the address for her studio and another quick search revealed it was a small house in a neighborhood on the edge of Oceanview bordering the city. She lived where she worked.

He sat back and stared at the image wondering if he should knock on her door first thing tomorrow and demand answers, or if he should watch from afar and see if she showed signs of pregnancy first. He quickly decided the latter was too close to stalking and he didn't want to wait longer than necessary to have answers anyway. Confronting her after breakfast was the course he would take.

Slamming his laptop shut he sipped at a blood bag and glared at his wall as he thought of how to best approach this human who could quite possibly be carrying his child.

CHAPTER FOUR

It had been a little over a week since the insemination and Chastity looked at her usual bowl of fruit and yogurt with a frown. She was hungry, but she didn't want this. She tried to ignore the niggling thoughts that she should take an early test. It was likely to give her a false result and she wasn't sure she could take the disappointment of that.

It was nearly eleven, a little late for breakfast, but she'd slept in after the late night at the library show where she'd been too nervous to eat any of the food, so she assumed that was why her stomach insisted it would rather have lunch now. She rummaged in the fridge and pulled out some leftover pork from a dinner she'd made her father a couple of nights ago and a jar of spicy pickles. She bit off a chunk of the pork to munch on as she reheated the rest, planning out her day. She wanted to work a few hours in the studio then maybe take a walk on the beach. She needed to distract herself so maybe she'd make a video for her account. She liked to offer painting tips online.

A sharp knock on the front door surprised her. She didn't get a lot of daytime visitors, most of her friends worked during the day and her father always called before popping in.

She padded across the house in her fuzzy cow slippers and matching pink pajama shorts and tank top. Her hair was in a messy bun, and she had no makeup on. When she opened the door expecting a package delivery, pickle in hand, she froze.

A vampire, and not just any vampire, this was the one from last night who had said such horrible things about her paintings. His blond curls were a halo around his stern face where reddish brown eyes glared at her. He wore a similar flower print shirt as last night, but it was paired with striped board shorts today. He looked like he'd woken up on the beach and strolled over, but why?

"Chastity Martin?" he asked, his eyes sweeping up and down her body with a frown.

Chastity wished she had a robe or sweater on, something she could pull close and hide from his scrutiny. "Um, yeah, can I help you with something?" She managed to keep her voice even, but she didn't smile.

"Are you pregnant?" he demanded.

If he'd said *I vant to suck your blood* she wouldn't have been as surprised as she was by that question. She stood there, mouth open, staring while he scowled.

"Excuse me?" she finally asked, sure she'd misheard him.

"I asked if you're pregnant."

"Well, I don't see how you have any right to that information, *Sir*." She snapped and moved to shut the door.

"Did you get inseminated at the Stonecroft Clinic last week?" he asked, freezing her just before the door fully shut.

Chastity swung the door back open. "How the fuck do you know that? Are you some kind of reporter?"

"No. I think I should come in," he said.

She wanted to say *fuck no*, but something told her she needed to hear whatever he'd come to tell her. She turned and walked to the living room assuming he'd follow. Her thoughts spun around what this could be about. Was he going to tell her that the clinic was in trouble, that he wanted her to join a class action lawsuit against them? Maybe she'd been injected with saline and not sperm at all and all her weird feelings were just psychosomatic.

"Are you a lawyer?" Chastity felt her blood begin to rush and her head spun. She nearly fell into the chair, fanning herself and gulping breaths. "What did the clinic do? Do I need to see a real doctor or get my money back?"

He shook his head. "My name is Viktor," he said, taking a seat as far from her as possible on a chair opposite the couch. He eyed her skeptically as she nodded and continued fanning herself and panting. "Are you okay?"

She shook her head. She was definitely not okay.

"Do you need some water?" he asked.

"Just tell me. Is the clinic in trouble for something? Should I get a lawyer?" She was hyperventilating now, and she tried to will herself down from the ledge of panic, but it was a losing battle. "Should I go to the emergency room?"

"You definitely need some water," he said and left the room, returning a few moments later with a glass of water from the kitchen. "Drink," he commanded, and she did.

When half the glass was gone, and she was breathing mostly normal again, she nodded to him. "Okay, spill. What horrible thing have they done?"

"That depends. Are you pregnant?"

She shook her head. "I don't know yet, it's too early to tell," she admitted, "but I still don't understand why you know I could be, and why you care."

Viktor took a deep breath and ran his hand through his curls. "Because if you are, then that baby is mine."

Relief, followed quickly by disbelief, washed through Chastity and she began to laugh. She held her arms over her belly and laughed hard. This had to be a prank, or a ridiculous mistake. "No," she said between bouts of laughter. "No, I am not a vampire."

He sneered at her. "I know you aren't a vampire; I'm not an idiot. But you *were* given my sperm. Felicity Stonecroft told me. It was a *Moon Goddess request*," he gritted and waved a hand in the air.

Ice cold fear crept up Chastity's spine and took all mirth out of the situation. "What the fuck?" she whispered.

"Exactly."

Chastity wasn't sure she could believe what he said, but she could tell that he believed it a hundred percent and that scared her. She also knew enough about vampires to know that family was extremely important to them. This guy would track his sperm carefully. No doubt he'd given it to the clinic with the intention of it being used with his permission. He wasn't just here to get her agreement in a lawsuit for misconduct. He was here to try and put a claim on her possible baby.

Chastity stood and started to pace the room. "Even if what you are saying is true and I was … inseminated with your sperm … Humans and vampires don't reproduce easily."

"I assure you it's possible, and with the Moon Goddess involved, things are more possible than usual. Are you pregnant?"

Chastity stopped in her pacing to glare at Viktor. "I already told you it's too early to tell."

"When will you know?"

"Another week at least."

Viktor stood and walked to the door. "I'll be back in a week," he said, and he left.

Two hours later Chastity was sitting across from Felicity who was smiling and twirling a lock of blonde hair. "Chastity, how are you feeling?"

"Scared shitless, did you inseminate me with vampire sperm?"

"Oh, yes. Did Viktor introduce himself to you? Such a nice

man and handsome too, don't you think?" She waggled her eyebrows at Chastity.

"Why?" Chastity demanded, not about to get sidetracked with a discussion of Viktor's physical attributes, which she *had* noticed of course. "Vampire sperm won't work; I wasted a cycle, and I refuse to be charged for this mix-up. I will consult a lawyer if I have to."

"This wasn't a mix-up, Chastity, this was divine intervention by the Moon Goddess and if you'll recall, you did sign a release that prohibits you from suing the company for interference by chaos-causing entities, it is the *Divine Intervention and Chaos Clause.*"

Chastity closed her eyes and took a calming breath. The Moon Goddess was definitely a chaos-causing entity. She was a lesser goddess who liked to meddle in human affairs more than most divine beings. "Humans rarely are able to have babies with vampires which makes this insemination likely to fail and I don't think I should be charged for the next round," she insisted, unwilling to assume it was going to work just because some goddess was involved.

Felicity rolled her eyes. "Not just any goddess, the Moon Goddess, Chastity, She picked you for this and it *will* be a successful insemination. You will have Viktor's baby, don't worry. It may be too early to test, but I have no doubt it took."

Chastity pinched the bridge of her nose in frustration. "Why would this be the will of the Moon Goddess?"

Felicity shrugged her shoulders. "That's not for me to know, I am merely a conduit of Her will when She chooses."

"And apparently I'm the vessel for Her desire to create chaos."

"You are a lucky girl," Felicity said with excitement. "Oh, while I have you, you're going to want to start taking these." She held out a bottle of blood supplements. "To support the growing fetus' blood needs. Otherwise, you'll start to crave raw meat which can be really tough on a human's digestion."

Not to mention my gag reflex, Chastity thought and wondered if the reason she'd taken a bite out of the cold pork that morning had been because of the fetus. "Right," she said, taking the pills and walking out of the office in a bit of a daze. She made it to her car before the tears started to fall.

She managed to drive herself bleary-eyed to Mooncalled Coffee. When Martha saw her walk in the door with red eyes and a runny nose, she rushed from behind the counter to embrace Chastity and led her to the office in the back.

"It didn't take?" she asked, handing Chastity a tissue. "It's okay, you'll try again, you knew this was a possibility."

"I don't know yet," Chastity said with a shaky breath. "The sperm was from a vampire."

"*Excuse* me?" Martha gasped.

"Yeah, some Viktor guy and he showed up at my house demanding to know if I'm pregnant. Apparently, it's the will of the fucking Moon Goddess."

"Oh Chastity," Martha sympathized and put an arm around her. "It's okay, this one will be a blip, the next insemination will work out."

Chastity shook her head. "What if this one does take?" she whispered her fear. "You know with witches and the Moon Goddess involved there's a high probability."

Martha didn't offer any rebuttal, just hugged Chastity tighter. "Have you talked to your dad?"

Chastity shook her head. "I'll call him when I get home." She knew her father would be supportive, no matter what, and she'd known Martha would be as well. She didn't have space in her life for people who were anything less, and maybe that was why she'd been short on boyfriends for so long and in this situation.

Would Viktor be a supportive figure in her life? Judging by her interactions with him so far, she doubted it.

CHAPTER FIVE

The next seven days were torture. All of Chastity's paintings took on a dark and anxious tone to the point that when her father stopped by to visit, he expressed concern over her well-being. He didn't see the possibility of a half vampire grandchild as a reason to fly off the edge, or so he'd told her.

She wasn't surprised by his supportive attitude and apparent eagerness to embrace a grandchild that might want to drink his blood. That was the type of man he had always been and it was exactly what she'd needed to hear while her thoughts and emotions spiraled with worry.

It was Friday morning when Chastity woke up and ran to the bathroom, vomiting up everything in her stomach. And she knew.

She was pregnant with a vampire's baby.

She touched her flat stomach as she lay on the bathroom floor and stared up at the ceiling. Happiness and fear mixed in a confusing swirl.

"It's okay, we'll figure this out and I will love you no matter what," she said, as much to assure herself as the growing life inside of her.

The sound of knocking on her front door told her that Viktor hadn't been kidding when he said he was coming back in a week for an answer. The man was punctual. She hated that she liked that.

She didn't want to face him right now. She wanted to marinate in her new certainty. She wanted to concentrate on the joy of becoming a mother. She didn't want the complications that he presented as the father figure she hadn't expected and didn't need.

She rinsed her mouth, threw on a robe and headed for the front door because she knew she had to deal with him whether she wanted to or not.

He was knocking again when she opened it and she glared at him. "It's early."

"Yeah, and it's time," he said holding up a bag.

"What's that?" she asked, but she was pretty sure she already knew.

"It's a test. I think we want to know as soon as possible, don't we?"

She grunted and grabbed the bag, then went to the kitchen to make some peppermint tea to hopefully settle her stomach. After she set the teapot on the stove, she turned to find Viktor had stopped at the entrance to the living room to stare at one of her recent paintings. It was one of her angry ones, dark colors and shapes that were harsh behind a half-hidden face of a woman.

She stiffened, ready to hear him tear it apart like he had the ones at the library show.

"Did you do this?" he asked, still staring at it.

"Yeah."

"It's different from your other work."

She glared at his back. "You've seen one themed show, how do you know what my work looks like," she snapped. It *was* different, but she wasn't going to admit it to him.

He turned, looking contrite. "I saw some of your stuff online too. I like this, it has a lot of feeling in it."

She wasn't sure what to do with that compliment, so she turned and readied her tea. "Tea?" she asked him, pulling down a cup.

"Sure," he answered and wandered into the living room.

When she came in to hand him his cup, he was staring at an older painting she'd done of two children on the beach. It was more realistic than she usually did, no elements of fantasy or abstraction.

"Is this Bleeker's Beach?"

"You know it?" She handed him his tea and he nodded.

"It was a favorite of mine as a kid."

"Me too," she said quietly. The children she'd painted into this one were supposed to be a reflection of her and the sibling she'd always wished she'd had. She sat down and sipped the still too hot liquid, wincing as her tongue burned because she'd never been good at waiting.

"So have you had any signs?" he asked as he sat. Like last time, he took the seat farthest from her and perched on the edge as if he were ready to escape.

"No," she lied. She wasn't sure why, but she wanted to see his reaction. She expected to see deep relief that she probably wasn't pregnant, but his face remained sternly blank.

"Well, are you ready to take the test?"

She wanted to say no to that too but knew it wouldn't do any good. Eventually she'd have to know and apparently so would he. She chugged a bit more of her tea and took the bag from him. He made a move as if he were going to follow her, but she gave him an incredulous look and he settled back down with a tinge of red to his cheeks.

"The test says it takes three to five minutes," he said.

"Well then, I will see you in five minutes," she mumbled as she walked to the bathroom which still smelled slightly of vomit.

. . .

Viktor stood and started pacing the living room as soon as the bathroom door closed. He wanted to follow her and stand over her. He wanted to make sure she was doing it right. He wanted to control whatever part of this insane situation he could.

He wasn't allowing himself to think about what he would do if it was positive. He couldn't fully accept it was a real possibility.

A part of him looked at Chastity and thought if it were a different situation he'd date her. Never seriously of course, she was a human. But still, she was attractive and talented, certainly the type of woman he enjoyed spending a little time with. He wouldn't have ever picked her for the role of mother of his child though. He'd never even considered a half human child as an option. What would their needs even be? He had heard of it happening, but it was so rare there wasn't much information out there about it.

It was only three minutes before Chastity came out of the bathroom, pale as a ghost and holding a little white stick in her hand.

"What is it?" he demanded.

"I'm pregnant," she whispered and looked up at him, her big green eyes misty and her plump bottom lip trembling.

She looked like she needed comfort and she was pregnant with his child, but all he could think about was how wrong this situation was and how trapped he suddenly felt. Viktor panicked.

He left the house without saying a word and jumped in his van.

He didn't stop to think until he was parked in front of his house. Even then he was pretty certain he'd been sitting there for a while just staring, mind blank. When his thoughts finally did spark, so did a sense of shame for the way he'd fled from Chastity who obviously could have used some comfort.

He had no idea how to handle this though. He was going to be a father, to a half human child and the mother was just some random woman who'd gotten his sperm by accident. Should he be expected to provide emotional support to her? No doubt he'd be providing some kind of financial support but anything beyond that couldn't be expected, could it?

It hadn't been in his plan, that was for sure. The plan *had* been, find a vampire couple to raise a child with. The woman would have all the emotional support provided by her partner and he'd just be extra for the kid.

He had a panicked thought about what his father was going to say when he found out. An artificial insemination baby with a vampire couple would have made the old vampire frown and grumble; but this? This was going to make him blow his top. That thought almost made Viktor smile. He lived to disappoint his controlling father.

His phone rang and he looked at his sister's name on the screen. She was not someone he wanted to talk to right now, but if he ignored her call, she'd just call right back. He took a steadying breath and answered. At least this would provide a distraction.

"Viktor, you never told me how you liked Chastity's art the other day. Janessa told me you were there and that she had a great show and has sold almost all her paintings displayed at the library already."

"It was interesting. How do you know Chastity?"

"I don't know her, but I know *of* her, and I have met her a couple of times at different galleries where she's been part of larger shows. She's a sweetheart, a little shy because she's new to showing herself off as an artist, but she has the talent so I'm sure she'll get over that fast. Did you meet her? You know, I actually think you two would get along. She's a free spirit, like you."

"She's human," he snapped.

"Woah, who spit in your coffee? You've dated humans before. I didn't suggest you knock her up and marry her for god's sake."

Viktor just hissed in response.

"Anyway, Lacey has a recital tomorrow night, and you haven't said if you're going to make it, she's been asking. She misses her Uncle Viktor."

"I'll be there." He couldn't disappoint his niece.

"Great, see you then."

Viktor hung up and ran a hand down his face. Chastity was already invading his life from multiple angles. How long would he be able to keep this goddess-caused chaos from being known by the entire world? Hopefully long enough for him to decide how he wanted to handle it in his personal life.

CHAPTER SIX

"Ginger has a recital tomorrow night. Come with, you could use a night out," Martha said as she served Chastity a slice of cake.

Chastity had dragged herself to the coffee shop after the horrid incident with Viktor and poured her soul out to her best friend.

"I don't know if I feel like socializing."

"It's tomorrow night, I'm sure you'll feel like it by then and if not, it will probably be best if you go anyway, and get out of your own head."

"You're probably right."

"Of course I'm right, I'm your best friend, no one knows what's best for you better than me."

"A sad but true fact, and why I'm in this situation. If I ever met a *man* I could be so honest with, I'd never let him go," Chastity laughed and put a hand on her belly.

"Hey, concentrate on that right there, the reason you did this. You get to be a mom finally, and the rest, well you really can't fight against the will of the Moon Goddess."

"So I've been told."

. . .

Chastity spent the next day and a half coming to terms with her pregnancy and wondering if she'd ever see Viktor again. Judging by the way he'd high-tailed it out of her house the morning before, she doubted he was going to fight for involvement. Which was fine with her, she'd never planned to have a father helping her. The whole point of the anonymous insemination was so she could do this on her own terms.

She wasn't planning to know so little about how to raise her child though. He or she would likely need a vampire influence. Maybe she'd join some kind of mom group for that.

It was all going to be okay she reminded herself over and over. This was a slight adjustment in her original plan and some learning needed to be done, but she was having a baby, and she was happy about that. There was a life growing inside of her even now, a life that was going to be hers to care for, love, and teach.

But not just hers, it would also be Viktor's, if he wanted to be involved. It wouldn't be an anonymous father who she'd specifically picked to look similar to herself. Would the child have Viktor's golden blond hair or her darker blonde locks, would it be curly like his or straight? Would the child have red-brown eyes and a penchant for blood? Or green eyes and an appetite that was easier for her to handle? It wasn't likely to be the spitting image of herself, but at least the father *was* handsome. She could admit that was a good thing.

Knowing that Martha was right, and she could use a distraction, Chastity got ready for the recital. A knock on the front door made her freeze just as she slipped her second sandal on. It had already become a familiar and foreboding sort of knock.

She stood stuck in indecision, wondering if he'd just go away if she was real quiet. She knew she wasn't likely to avoid Viktor forever though, and maybe he was going to apologize for running out yesterday. That would be nice.

She tried to expect positive and opened the door with a slight frown on her face and her purse in hand. She wanted it to be obvious that she was getting ready to leave so he wouldn't think she was about to invite him in for a long conversation.

Viktor stood there not with a look of contrition but one of determination. Which had her ready to go on the defensive.

"What can I do for you?" she asked, not moving to let him in.

"I came to apologize," he said with no hint of remorse in his tone.

"Okay," she prompted.

"We should talk about how this is going to work."

Chastity was dumbfounded. Did he actually think that constituted an apology? She crossed her arms over her chest and raised an eyebrow.

"Do you think we should get some kind of agreement drawn up, something legal?"

Chastity narrowed her eyes at the vampire, he wanted some kind of custody agreement? He was a sperm donor, what the hell was he thinking?

"I think you should leave. I have somewhere to be." And apparently, she needed to make a phone call to the Stonecroft Clinic and see what, if any, rights this vampire had over her child. Admittedly, this was something she should have asked the last time she'd been in there, but she'd been far too distracted by the confirmation that they'd intentionally inseminated her with vampire sperm to ask logical follow up questions. She stepped onto the porch forcing him to back up and closed her door behind her.

"Where are you going?" he demanded.

"I don't think that is any of your business. I'd say thanks for stopping by but I'm not really glad you did," she snapped and walked past him to her car.

Satisfaction filled her at leaving him the way he'd left her yesterday; sudden and without explanation.

"Chastity, we need to talk about this situation," he said, following her.

"You're right, but we don't have to talk now. Pregnancies last about forty weeks so we have time." She paused and turned to him. "Are vampire pregnancies shorter?"

"No. Have you been to the doctor? Have you gotten a due date? Are you healthy? What about blood?"

His intrusive questions irritated her. She turned away from him and scanned for nosy neighbors listening in. She glared at Mrs. Layton who was watering her sidewalk next door.

Great, the whole town was about to know she was pregnant with a vampire's baby.

She continued to her car and got in without answering him. As she backed out of the driveway with more speed than necessary, she got a lot of satisfaction out of the fact that he was standing there watching her go with his jaw hanging wide. As she drove away, she looked in the rearview mirror and spotted a VW van parked near her house. It was mint green and had a paisley pattern trailing down from the roof.

Damnit, she loved it, and she hated to love anything about the vampire.

When she parked outside the dance school fifteen minutes later, she was feeling good about herself. She took a moment to apply some lipstick then groaned when she saw the same VW van pull into the lot.

Had he followed her?

She got out of the car and stalked toward his van, ready to tell him to go to hell with his demands. But when he stepped out, a gorgeous woman threw herself at him with a squeal of delight.

Chastity wasn't about to wait around and see any more of that. She turned and hurried into the building, praying she'd avoid Viktor and his girlfriend for the rest of the night.

"Chastity! Over here," Martha called out and waved her arms. She was sitting in the front along with two rows of family all here to watch Ginger dance. The large show of family support brought instant tears to Chastity's eyes. She didn't have an extended family, it was just her and her father. Her child would never look out in a crowd and see this kind of support. She swiped at the tears as she hurried to sit next to Martha knowing it was stupid to cry over something impossible to change.

"Oh no, hormones already working their magic, huh?"

"I think so."

Martha put an arm around her and she leaned into it, hoping to disappear in the crowd. Maybe she'd make an excuse and sneak out before it was over so she wouldn't risk running into Viktor.

Martha's eighty-year-old grandmother, Elaine, was sitting on her other side and put a hand to her shoulder. "What's got you so upset?"

"Nothing, it's fine, Elaine," Chastity assured her at the same time Martha said.

"She's fine, Grandma."

"No, she's not, that look comes from one of two things. Either you're pregnant, or you had a fight with a man."

"Or both," Chastity mumbled too low for the eighty-year-old's supernatural hearing to pick up. "I just had a hard day, my painting didn't turn out," she assured the woman louder.

Elaine didn't look convinced but nodded. "Well, it'll all work out. I commune with the Moon Goddess you know, and She's got Her spirit on you. I can sense it."

Chastity shifted uncomfortably, hadn't that crazy witch at the clinic said something about the Moon Goddess? She should have run straight to Martha with that, werewolves were particularly fond of the Moon Goddess and her antics.

Martha was giving her a thorough look and nodding. "I see it too, Gran."

"Great, well maybe one of you can tell Her She's latched onto the wrong womb."

Elaine laughed loud, drawing a lot of attention to their group and Chastity tried to hide her face, hoping Viktor wasn't close enough to see.

"The Moon Goddess doesn't usually get involved with vampire affairs," Martha said.

"Who said anything about a vampire?" Elaine said loudly.

Chastity groaned and shrunk down further in her seat, regretting her decision to come here. Thankfully the lights dimmed then and the show began. Chastity was lost for a while in the joy of seven-year-olds dancing across the stage. With no intermission in the dancing, she had no chance to make excuses to leave early, although eventually the lights were back on and everyone was moving.

"I need to go. Tell Ginger she was amazing."

Martha gave her a little frown. "You aren't staying for the reception? There will be cookies and juice."

"No, I'm tired. Hormones you know." She was going to love this excuse for the next few months to avoid anything she didn't really want to do.

"I get that, okay come by the shop tomorrow. We need to talk about the Moon Goddess."

"I will." She waved goodbye to the rest of the large werewolf family. Elaine had fallen asleep during the performance and was yipping quietly, slumped back in her seat. Chastity thankfully avoided any shouted goodbyes from the half-deaf werewolf that would draw attention to her.

She kept her head down as she made her way out of the auditorium.

"Hey, Chastity Martin, right?"

Chastity froze at the sound of her name.

"The artist, right?" the woman asked as she hurried into Chastity's field of vision.

Chastity wanted to curse at the sight of the cute little blonde vampire. It was the woman who had flung herself at Viktor in the parking lot. But how did the woman know her name? And what she did for a living? Had Viktor told his girlfriend about her? Was this woman about to introduce herself as the future stepmother of Chastity's child?

She put a protective hand to her belly.

The blonde stared at her with a huge smile. "You are her, right? I met you at a couple of different art galleries, you likely don't remember me at all," she laughed. "Just another random fan."

Chastity relaxed slightly, maybe this was just a fan who happened to be dating the father of her unborn child, and if she was quick, she'd avoid the awkward encounter with Viktor.

"Yes, I am her, or uh, I'm Chastity Martin," she fumbled.

"I just love your work. I wanted to talk to you about commissioning something for an outdoor play area. My husband and I have been talking about making it special and I think you are the perfect person to do that."

Chastity wanted to puke at the word husband. Viktor was married, and this beautiful bubbly creature was his wife. Chastity was certain she hadn't spotted a ring on Viktor's finger but that could just be because he didn't like jewelry, or didn't like to look taken. So why was his sperm at the clinic if he was married? Maybe this woman was infertile and they wanted to raise a child with another couple and now, she was that other couple. Chastity was going to have to share her child not just with Viktor but with this woman too.

Bile rose in her throat and anxiety had her heart beating wildly, then her head started to spin. "I really need to be going," she groaned.

"Oh yes dear, you don't look well. Expect a call from me. I'll get your number from Janessa!"

Chastity waved a hand she hoped was polite and ran from the room.

. . .

Viktor walked up to his sister with Lacey on his back, a cookie clutched in her hand.

"Oh Viktor, you just missed her."

"Missed who?"

"Chastity Martin."

Viktor darted his gaze around. "Chastity is here?"

"Was. She ran out looking sick, poor thing. I really do want you to meet her, I think she's just adorable."

"We've met," Viktor said with a frown.

"Oh, well am I right? Perfect match for a fun date or two?"

"No," Viktor said and set Lacey down. "I have to go, munchkin," he said to his niece then kissed his sister's cheek and hurried out to the parking lot just in time to see Chastity's VW beetle speed out of the parking lot.

How had he missed that she was here, and whose kid was she watching? He hated that there was so much he didn't know about the woman having his baby. And judging by the way she'd practically run to get away from him earlier, he had a feeling it wasn't going to be easy to remedy that.

But she would just have to get over her disappointment in having a father for her child. After all, she wasn't the only one in this unwillingly and they needed to be adults about it. A serious talk about how this parenting situation was going to work was necessary, and he was going to make that happen sooner rather than later.

Viktor got in his van and headed back to Chastity's place. He knocked on the door ready to demand that they talk things through no matter how uncomfortable it was for them both.

When she answered the door his determination deflated. She was looking pale and glassy-eyed.

"What is wrong with you?" Fear made his words rougher than he intended.

"I'm pregnant," she snapped, then covered her mouth. Eyes wide, she turned and hurried away from the door.

He was sure she wasn't alright, so he followed her to the bathroom where she was leaning over the toilet heaving. His heart softened for her at this obvious sign of pregnancy and the suffering she was going through. He remembered his sister complaining nonstop for the first four months of her pregnancy about the constant nausea and daily puking.

"Can I get you anything?"

She stiffened at his voice, obviously she hadn't heard him follow. "Some tea, peppermint," she whispered into the toilet bowl.

He went to the kitchen, thankful for a task that made him feel helpful. By the time the tea was ready Chastity was shuffling to the kitchen having changed into a pair of pajama pants and a large t-shirt, both splattered in paint.

"Thanks," she said, taking the tea and moving to the living room where she curled up on the chair. She was so small, and he worried about her ability to handle months of what her body was already putting her through.

He sat on the couch and waited for her to acknowledge him before he tried to talk to her.

"Why are you here?" she asked after taking a few hesitant sips and sucking in air at the obvious burn of the too-hot liquid.

He kept his voice soft, none of the judgment he knew had been covering his anxiety earlier. "I think we have a lot to discuss, don't you?"

She shook her head. "This isn't what I was planning."

That answer grated on him, as if this was anything even close to resembling what he'd planned for his sperm. "Me neither, but here we are."

She sighed heavily and took another sip of her tea, still obviously too hot judging by the way she winced after the sip.

"It's hot, let it cool," he snarled and she glared at him as she took another sip just to spite him.

"So what is it you want out of this, Viktor?"

"Just let me be a part of it. I want to know the child and I want to experience some of this journey with you." He wanted to point out how unfair it all was, how his sperm was basically stolen, how she wasn't his choice and how wrong this all was. But looking at her, obviously struggling and sipping slowly on a cup of tea he'd made her, he couldn't deny she was just as much a victim in this as he was. She likely had chosen some anonymous human donor that she thought would make a perfect little baby for her to love, all by herself. But she'd gotten him, a vampire who was very much aware that it was his child growing in her womb.

She closed her eyes and nodded. "Okay, I have a doctor's appointment next week. If you want to tag along, that would be fine."

He jumped up, eager to take what she was offering and not push for more, not yet anyway. "Great, here's my number. Call or text with the details." He handed her a card with his name and number on it.

"Thanks," she said as she took the card, but he wasn't sure he believed she was thankful for anything he was doing to push into her life. Well, the feeling was mutual, because he didn't want to be thankful for any little part of her life she was letting him be in. Could they build a relationship on mutual discontent?

"I don't blame you for being upset about this, I am too. And I'm not convinced that child is going to turn out okay half human, there's so little known about these situations." He shook his head and took a breath because her face was starting to twist in a way that made him fear she was about to cry, and he wasn't sure he could handle that. His voice was softer as he continued. "But here we are, and I won't have my child out there not knowing its father. Even if it is half human."

Her voice was rough with emotion as she replied. "Felicity seems to think a half human vampire child will be fine. She put me on some blood supplements." Chastity shrugged.

"That's likely what has you puking so much. Your human stomach isn't made for that stuff."

She glared at him, "And what, in your professional opinion, should I do, Viktor?" she snapped and he was glad to see her switch from sad to mad, mad he could handle.

"I *am* a professional when it comes to blood, Chastity, *I'm* the vampire here," he snapped back.

"That doesn't qualify you to tell me what to do, you're not a pregnant human with a half vampire fetus."

He glared at her. "Fine, I'll see you next week for the appointment."

"Great," she said, not standing to walk him out.

Viktor paused at the front door. "If you need anything before then, you have my number, and I'd appreciate having yours." He left without waiting for her response. He knew he hadn't kept his cool, but she grated on him in a way he wasn't used to.

CHAPTER SEVEN

Chastity wanted to throw her cup at him as he shut the door, but she didn't want to clean up the mess it would make. What an annoying vampire. He had the audacity to come in here making demands and trying to tell her what was best for her. He—well she had to admit he probably did know more about blood and the way it reacted in the body than she did, but still.

She looked at his card. It was for a surf shop she'd walked past many times on the beach. She hadn't realized it was vampire-owned. No wonder he had a slight tan and dressed like a beach bum; he *was* a beach bum.

"I wanted a successful, athletic human and I got a beach bum vampire," she groaned.

She walked to the kitchen and stuck the card to her fridge, in no rush to give him her number in return.

The next day she sat outside Mooncalled and sipped tea, staring at the bran muffin Martha had insisted on putting in front of her. She wasn't sure her stomach could handle it. She took a nibble and set it back down, waiting for rejection. She hadn't held down her breakfast that morning, so she was starving, but at the same time nauseous. "This is fun," she whispered.

"Okay, the men have it handled in there for a minute," Martha said, sitting down across from her and eyeing the uneaten muffin with a frown. "Are you managing anything in your stomach?"

"Not really," Chastity admitted.

"Well, do what you can and talk to the doctor, maybe there's something else you should be doing since it's, you know," Martha used her fingers to indicate fangs in her mouth and Chastity laughed.

"Maybe I need to eat a rare steak or liver or something."

"Sounds like what I crave," Martha said.

"Tell me about the Moon Goddess. Felicity at the clinic said she was following the orders of the Moon Goddess and so I couldn't sue over the mistake."

"*Divine Intervention and Chaos Clause*," Martha said with a nod. "Most places have that nowadays."

"So why me, and why a vampire?"

"That's a good question and I don't know, but I think maybe if you commune with Her, you might find out."

"Commune with the Moon Goddess?" Chastity was doubtful, she wasn't a spiritual person and she was pretty sure communing with goddesses involved being naked in the woods. "Do I really want more of Her attention on me?"

"Yes. She is the only one who has the answers you want. I will plan it all, just show up," Martha begged. "I promise it will be fun even if She doesn't feel like answering your call."

Chastity couldn't say no when her friend looked that excited to do something for her. "Okay."

Martha beamed with excitement. "We should do it soon, since it might help you feel better, how about tomorrow night?"

Chastity just nodded and forced down another small bite of the bran muffin. If a little naked communing would make eating possible, she'd agree.

. . .

Chastity spent two days staring at Viktor's business card every time she passed through the kitchen. Should she call him? Should she give him her number? He knew where she lived. He could stop by any time if he wanted. Maybe having her number would keep him from showing up unannounced. Did she want that?

By the time she was getting ready to go commune with the Moon Goddess she was happy to be leaving the house and walking away from that damn card and the feeling that she was being immature.

He *was* the father of this child and all he was asking for was involvement. But he was so pushy, aggravating, and cute. Fuck, she hated how cute he was, how much she knew that if the situation were different, she'd willingly date him briefly.

Martha and Glen lived on a large plot of land on the south end of Oceanview not only because they had a lot of kids who needed space, but so they could do some minor hunting and carousing in wolf form when they wanted. And apparently so they could dance naked around a bonfire to commune with the Moon Goddess.

Martha and Elaine met her in the driveway with hugs and excitement, both wearing robes and rubber boots. Yep, this was going to be a naked event.

"Did you tell her?" Chastity whispered to Martha as they hugged hello.

"Only that you want to know why the Moon Goddess is watching you."

Chastity followed them through a well-worn trail into the woods to a cleared space with a small fire already burning.

"Glen and Benjamin were out here earlier, got things set up for us," Martha explained as she dropped her robe and slipped off her boots. Elaine did the same and Chastity tried not to look. Neither woman was ashamed of their bodies, one old and frail, the other round and firm with new life.

Chastity was slower, slipping off her tennis shoes then taking off her t-shirt and sweats. She wasn't ashamed of her body, but being naked outside wasn't something she was used to.

"Come here, dear," Elaine beckoned her forward with an encouraging smile.

When Chastity was next to Elaine, she opened a small bag and pulled out a necklace which she slipped over Chastity's head. It was made with a thick leather cord and hanging from it was a large stone with the phases of the moon etched on it. Next, Elaine opened a vial of liquid and dabbed it on Chastity's forehead. It smelled like frankincense and pine.

"This will help open your mind and focus your thoughts. The Moon Goddess will either choose to enlighten you or not, but you have to listen, or you could miss it."

Chastity settled on a mat Martha had laid out for her near the fire and stared into the flames, trying to clear her mind and just be open to anything the Moon Goddess might want to share. It was hard to not ask questions or demand answers but to just wait for whatever knowledge the fickle goddess might want to offer. Somehow Chastity managed it.

She wasn't sure how long she sat there staring at the flames as they danced but eventually the random flames started to take shape. She saw the figure of a woman with a rounded belly, and then a baby. Both coming and going so swiftly she certainly would have missed it if she'd blinked.

And that was it. "Well fuck, I already knew I was pregnant," Chastity grumbled.

"You're pregnant!" Elaine gasped with excitement.

Chastity cursed herself for forgetting the old woman was near.

"Well, who the hell is the father? I didn't think you were seeing anyone," Elaine encouraged.

"I'm not—there isn't—it's complicated," Chastity trailed off, unsure what to say. She'd been prepared to tell people she was a strong independent woman who was having a baby on her own. She was not prepared to explain she was giving birth to a human-vampire hybrid whose father was someone she barely knew and had never even dated.

"Not your business, Gran," Martha said. "What did you see in the flames, Chastity?"

"Just a pregnant woman and then a baby."

"Well, there's your answer, you are going to have a healthy baby, no worries," Elaine said with a clap.

How could Chastity complain about that? She wanted a baby, and this was a sign that she'd have that. It just didn't answer any of her questions about why it was with a vampire and what kind of things she should expect with raising a half-vampire half-human child. But really most importantly, why her?

She met Martha's gaze and tried to be comforted with the fact that the Moon Goddess apparently was assuring her of a healthy child in a few months. The details of the child's father and future eating habits would be dealt with when the time came, she supposed.

"Come in for some tea," Elaine said as she pulled on her robe.

Chastity dressed and followed Elaine to the house, Martha squeezed her arm reassuringly. "You know, despite the goddess' predilection for causing trouble, She also does things with purpose. And I think this little bundle serves a purpose." Martha laid a hand on Chastity's stomach.

"I think it's chaos," Chastity said with a laugh, "But I will love it anyway."

"All children are chaos," Martha laughed as her two youngest came barreling out of the house dressed as superheroes shooting each other with soft darts. Twins, Silvia and Sam. "But I love them," Martha said even as she caught a dart in the arm.

"Hey now, all superheroes get ready for bed," Glen said, coming out of the house. He embraced his wife as the children ran back inside with groans. "How did it go out there?"

"Wonderful. Chastity is pregnant and it's going to be healthy," Elaine announced.

Glen had already known, so there was no surprise in his face, only relief. A healthy child was all she should be worried about as well. She knew that and she was filled with guilt because she *wasn't* just thankful, she was also angry that it wasn't all happening the way she'd carefully planned.

After a cup of tea and lots of unwanted advice from Elaine about pregnancy and child rearing, Chastity headed home. When she lay in bed later with one hand on her flat belly she thought about Viktor and wondered if he'd be relieved or angry that the goddess was promising a healthy child.

CHAPTER EIGHT

Chastity continued to just look at Viktor's card while debating with herself if she should tell him about the vision. She didn't really want to talk to him, and she wasn't sure how he would feel about communing with goddesses. Some people were staunchly against it because it so often backfired when you invited the divine to take a closer look at you. Of course that boat had already sailed for them because for whatever reason, the Moon Goddess had chosen them to bear this act of chaos.

After four days of walking past it she was standing in front of the fridge, cup of yogurt in her hand. She ate and glared at the card. She wondered what he'd been doing these last few days. Had his life changed at all? She knew he wasn't puking his guts out all day like her, but she would be happy to know he at least had some stress-induced heartburn.

"I'm glad he's giving me space," she said firmly and turned from the fridge. She was glad he wasn't stopping by randomly and couldn't call or text. But every time she thought she heard a car stop outside her house she waited; breath held for a loud knock. None came and every time, the slight disappointment made her angry. She didn't need or want him intruding on her life. That wasn't what this was supposed to be.

The next day she got a phone call from the vampire who she was certain was his wife, Persia Lane, and she cringed as she agreed to meet the woman to discuss a painting commission. But the address Persia gave wasn't the one on Viktor's card which meant he hadn't even given her his personal information, just his business, and that made her unnecessarily angry.

She doubted Persia had told Viktor about hiring her, which meant this was bound to be an awkward interaction but now more than ever, Chastity couldn't turn down paid work. And maybe she had a twisted desire to check out his wife and private space.

She drove to Persia's house in the city that day. Persia wanted a mural done on an inner garden wall which was something that Chastity thought would be an incredibly fun thing to do. Another reason why she didn't turn it down. When Chastity pulled up to the house, she sat in her car for a few minutes, gathering her nerves.

This was a mansion, Viktor was rich. Maybe he wasn't a full-time beach bum, maybe he was also something fancy like a lawyer or a doctor. Maybe his family had money, and he was just a spoiled trust fund baby. She decided that was the most likely scenario.

She studied the house. This could be a place where her child would spend time in the future, how the hell was Chastity supposed to compete?

She had been relieved when she thought that Viktor worked and lived at the surf shack. It was comparable to her own home and studio. She thought maybe they were similar in ways they'd discover later on and raise up this child in equal settings, but this … this was something else.

Fear over the future threatened to overwhelm Chastity for a moment but she pulled herself together because she was a professional. She grabbed her sketchbook and got out of her car. She may not have this kind of money, but the love she'd have for her child would more than make up for any luxury she couldn't afford. She'd wanted this child so much she'd gone out and gotten it, Viktor was just unfortunately caught up in its creation.

"Chastity Martin!" Persia squealed as she hurried out of the house. She was dressed in a long black summer dress, her pale skin nearly glistening in the sun and her blonde hair pulled back in a perfect ponytail. Diamonds glinted at her ears and neck. She was truly stunning and made Chastity feel like a frump in her sundress.

Chastity knew she looked fine, and she wasn't usually self-conscious about fashion choices. But knowing this was Viktor's wife put her automatically on the defensive.

"I am so excited to have you here for this," Persia said.

Chastity shoved her anxiety down further and pulled all her professionalism forward as she greeted Persia. "I'm happy to be here," she assured Persia as the woman embraced her briefly. It occurred to Chastity then that if Persia didn't already know about the baby, that when she did find out this could make things very awkward. She suddenly wanted to have never agreed to this, but she couldn't turn and run now, it would only make her look ridiculous. They were all adults, and they were all going to have to live within each other's lives to some degree, might as well make it as peaceful and friendly as possible. "I'm anxious to see the wall you want painted. I can really visualize once I see the whole space," she prompted. Maybe if she kept things super professional it would help when everything came out.

"Oh yes, come around this way. It's going to be a surprise for my daughter, that's why I wanted you to come now, she's at dance class."

Chastity followed and Persia talked on and on as she walked. Chastity caught a couple of words, *brother* and *free spirit* but she couldn't pay attention. Persia and Viktor already had a child.

Why hadn't Viktor mentioned that he was a father already? Probably the same reason he hadn't mentioned he had a wife. He was ashamed of what they were creating, ashamed that he'd be having a half human child with her.

This disaster was just getting more complicated.

"Here it is," Persia announced as she stopped behind the house, throwing her hands out to indicate a plain brick wall under an awning that covered half of a large garden and grassy play area.

It was really a beautiful spot, perfect for kids to play and Chastity had to bite her lip to keep from tearing up. Her own backyard was a quarter of this size and didn't offer the kind of shade that a vampire child might need.

"Oh, are you alright?" Persia asked, coming close and touching Chastity's arm.

"Yes, it's just … allergies. I must be allergic to one of these flowers blooming."

Persia looked around with a frown. "Will that be a problem? I can have anything removed that you need so you can work here comfortably."

Fuck, she was nice too. Chastity couldn't dislike her even though she *really* wanted to. "I think I'll be okay. So tell me what you're thinking for this wall."

Chastity pulled out a sketch pad as she listened to Persia explain a scene of oversize flowers and mushrooms with children playing among them.

"I want it to have an Alice in Wonderland feel to it. Do you think you can do that?"

"I'm certain I can." She couldn't help a little glee at knowing Viktor would hate it. It was just the sort of whimsical thing she'd done for the library show that he'd had such nasty things to say about.

"Great, why don't you spend a few minutes getting acquainted with the space. I'm going to fetch some refreshments."

As soon as Persia left, Chastity settled into a chair and began to sketch some ideas. She was lost in the art and didn't even notice that she was no longer alone until he was right beside her.

"What on earth are you doing here?"

Chastity jumped up and dropped her sketchbook and pencils.

"Viktor," she gasped.

"Oh good, you're here." Persia said as she walked out with a tray of lemonade.

"Why are you here?" Viktor questioned again.

"Don't be rude, Viktor. I asked Chastity to do a mural, it's a surprise for Lacey."

"Really," Viktor said with a raised eyebrow.

"If it's a problem, I don't have to do it," Chastity said quickly, not wanting to be the reason these two fought.

"Why the hell would it be a problem, and Viktor's feelings on it certainly don't matter," Persia scoffed but softened the blow with a kiss to his cheek before turning back to Chastity. "Lemonade?"

Chastity accepted the drink and Viktor picked up her sketchbook.

"Is this your idea?" he asked her.

Chastity's body stiffened with defensiveness. "It's what Persia and I discussed, just some ideas, but if you have a different direction you would like to see—"

"He's not in charge," Persia interrupted. "No matter how much he hates that he's not," she added with a laugh.

"Well, I think it's important that everyone agrees," Chastity tried. The dynamic between the two vampires was confusing and she wanted away from it.

"My husband and I already discussed this, it's perfect," Persia said, sending a glare to Viktor.

"Okay, well why don't you take a look at these then," Chastity said carefully and motioned to the sketchbook still clutched in Viktor's hand.

Persia reached out and made a gimme motion at Viktor who rolled his eyes and handed it to her.

Chastity wasn't sure what was going on here, but their relationship didn't seem great. She knew that she and the child would just be complicating things for them and that didn't bode well for the child's wellbeing here. She needed to think about talking to a lawyer, her first priority was the child's health and safety, that included its emotional care.

"Maybe I should go, you and your husband could discuss and get back to me. I'm happy to work up a few more ideas and we can discuss everything before I start."

"Nonsense. Since my brother is here, I think we should enjoy a bit of a snack together. I have Terry making some sandwiches and fruit to go with this lemonade."

"Oh, I don't think I need to stick around to meet your brother," Chastity said with a nervous laugh. She didn't want to be any more involved with this situation than she already was, and something about the way Persia said brother made Chastity feel like this was a setup. What had she jabbered about earlier, a *free spirit?* Was this some kind of ploy to get her dating someone in the family now that she was having Viktor's baby?

"Well too late for that," Persia laughed.

"I'm her brother," Viktor said. "Did you think I was the husband?" he laughed.

Chastity glared at him. "Well for as much as I know about you, why wouldn't I assume the woman who you hugged outside the dance recital and whose backyard you showed up in was your wife?" she snapped.

"Woah, what did I miss?" Persia asked.

"Nothing," they both responded, and Persia crossed her arms, narrowing her eyes at them both.

"And yet you accepted the invitation here," Viktor accused.

"As if I can turn down a job at this point," she snapped then shook her head and heaved a breath. "I think I should go. Do let me know what you think of the sketches, Persia. If you still want it done I'd be happy to do the work."

Persia looked suspiciously at Viktor, and Viktor scowled at Chastity.

Chastity hurried away before anything more mortifying could be said.

"Chastity, wait," Viktor yelled, stopping her right as she got to her car.

"I didn't know she was your sister."

"No, you thought she was my wife? And you thought it would be a good idea to come here and what? Check out the competition?"

"Competition?" she scoffed. "You think I care if you're involved with someone? This situation isn't romantic, Viktor. It isn't even intentional! I just wanted the job."

Viktor sighed and ran a hand through his curls. "Okay, okay, that wasn't fair. But it really threw me off to find you here."

"Likewise."

"You haven't called."

"I was going to today," she lied, "I have an appointment tomorrow morning at an OB-GYN the Stonecroft Clinic recommends."

"I'll be there."

"Are you going to tell her?"

"Isn't it too early to tell people?"

"Yeah, I guess so." She didn't mention that she'd gotten confirmation from the Moon Goddess that the pregnancy would be fine.

"Have you told anyone?"

"My father and my best friend know. It's not like I'm going around announcing it, just telling the people who I need for support right now no matter how it turns out."

"I can support you too," he reminded.

"Right, I haven't forgotten your desire to draw up a contract," she said stiffly.

"Chastity," he hissed. "What the hell am I supposed to do? It would have been drawn up before insemination if things had gone the proper way."

She shrugged. "I don't know, it's not like I've done this before, and I didn't look into vampire sperm donor customs, sorry," she sneered.

He pursed his lips and gave a sharp nod. "I'll see you tomorrow."

Chastity pulled out of the driveway sure she'd never hear from Persia again about the mural, which was too bad. She'd been excited to do something on such a large scale. The money wouldn't have hurt either.

Viktor walked back to find Persia sitting in front of a tray of sandwiches and fruit, sipping a blood bag.

"What the fuck was that?" she demanded.

Viktor dropped into a chair and popped a grape into his mouth. "*That* is complicated."

"Right, so you know her, obviously. Did you sleep with her? Is that why that was so awkward?"

"Worse," he said and leaned forward with his head in his hands.

"Did you bite her?" Persia asked, a gasp of scandal in her tone.

"Even worse than that," he sighed. He wasn't sure if it was the right time to tell his sister, wasn't there was some kind of ten-week rule about viable fetuses and sharing pregnancy news? Chastity's words rattled around in his head. *They are people who will support me no matter what happens.* He knew his sister would be that for him. "She's pregnant."

"Oh, well maybe don't date her then I guess. Sorry, I thought she was single when I decided you two would make a good match."

"She is single," he took a deep breath. "Which is why she went to the Stonecroft Clinic and got inseminated. But that psychotic witch, Felicity, listened to the Moon Goddess and used my sperm." He spewed it quickly and a weight lifted off his chest.

"No way," Persia said after a few shocked moments of silence.

"Way."

"Dude, you're going to be a dad. To a half human! How does that even work?"

"I'm hoping we will find out more from the doctor tomorrow."

"So you're going to be involved?"

"As much as possible. That was the whole idea behind giving my sperm to the bank in the first place. I wanted to parent part time. I just planned to have a say in with who. I also thought it would involve more than a single woman, that puts a lot of pressure on me." He sighed heavily even though he knew his sister was thinking he was being overly dramatic. "This was not what I asked for."

"The *Divine Intervention and Chaos Clause*," she said with a frown.

"Exactly."

Persia gave him a sly smile. "She's pretty though, and talented, too."

"Don't," Viktor warned.

"What?"

"I don't think getting involved with her is a good idea so just get that out of your mind."

"You're right, being involved with the mother of your child would be just a terrible thing, wouldn't it? You know, when she gets super horny in her second trimester maybe I'll introduce her to James' business partner, you know, Benton, the one who likes to golf?"

"I would drive a stake through your heart and his, Persia, if you put Chastity anywhere near that asshole."

Persia laughed.

Viktor stayed long enough to greet Lacey when she got home from dance class then headed back to the beach. He had some late afternoon surf lessons scheduled and thanks to Persia's second trimester comment, too many disturbing thoughts were running through his mind.

He threw himself into the physicality of his lessons, the last of which was with a cute vampire about his age. The sun was just setting as they began.

Right away he picked up on all the signs that this woman was interested in more than just a lesson in surfing. She was dressed in a tiny silver bikini which was in no way meant for the kind of movement surfing would entail, and she got close to him as often as possible, giggling and fluttering her lashes, even flashing her fangs.

Usually he'd take up the offer without a thought. He'd end the lesson early, bring her back to his place and fuck her hard, maybe twice, then give her a blood bag refresher and send her on her way telling her that the next lesson would be ten percent off.

Usually he wouldn't get irritated by the thought that Chastity could do this same dance with some random guy in her second trimester when her hormones were out of control and making her want release anywhere she could find it.

"Wow, that was harder than I expected," the woman whose name he couldn't quite remember said as they dragged their boards back to the shop. "I think I need something to drink," she hinted, her eyes flitting to his neck.

She met his gaze expectantly and he knew this was the part where she expected him to invite her up for a drink neither of them really wanted. She was running a hand along her toned stomach and all it did was remind him that Chastity was pregnant with his child, and he'd never even touched her intimately.

"There's a bar right down the beach there," he said, turning away to lock up the boards.

She huffed an annoyed sound then grabbed her things and stomped off.

Viktor leaned his head against the door to the board storage. What the hell was wrong with him? He turned to call the woman back, to do what he usually did. Why did the goddess's decision have to ruin his life? Why did it have to change anything? He'd always intended to have a child with someone he didn't love and wouldn't have a relationship with. That had always been the plan.

But as he stared at the woman's retreating back, still unable to recall her name, he said nothing.

His phone dinged inside with a message and he hurried to it.

10:30 appointment.

Also your sister called, she wants me to start as soon as possible on the mural, but I won't do it if it will bother you.

He hesitated over responding. He wasn't sure how he felt about Chastity becoming involved in his sister's life, it felt intrusive. And yet he knew he couldn't tell her that, it would make him look like an asshole.

I'll be there.

Do the mural, she's excited about it.

CHAPTER NINE

Chastity went to Mooncalled Coffee the next morning to tell Martha everything that had happened with Viktor and his sister. They settled at an outdoor table and Chastity sipped tea while she unloaded all of the new drama. "I'm excited about the mural, it's going to be fun and I need the money, now more than ever," she touched her stomach. "So I'm doing it. If it's a little awkward, oh well. I mean … what are the chances he'll ever be there when I'm painting?"

"How do you feel about seeing him at the appointment today?"

"Weird. I expected to do this stuff alone, maybe with my dad or you. It feels honestly a little intrusive. He's never so much as seen me in a bathing suit and I'm likely to be half naked on that table."

"Just wait till the birth when you're all naked, sweaty, and screaming."

"Thanks for that image."

Martha smiled wide, showing her large canine teeth. "It's a beautiful thing, but it's not pretty to watch."

"Well, I'm not sure he needs to be there for that anyway."

"Right, like he's going to want to miss it. He intended his sperm to create a child he's involved with. Don't forget you're dealing with another species here, this isn't a human one-night stand."

"I should have just gone the traditional drunken take-home-from-the-bar route for pregnancy," Chastity grumbled.

"Chastity?"

Both women swiveled their heads around to see Viktor standing at the café entrance. He looked like he'd been out in the water early that morning, skin still sticky with salt water, shorts mostly dry thanks to the heat of the early day and bits of sand stuck to them. He had a tank top on and a lot of bare skin was showing. Chastity couldn't help noticing how wide and muscular his shoulders were, they'd been hidden every other time in his button up flower shirts.

"Viktor?" she asked, feeling dumb for sounding like she wasn't sure this was the guy who was fathering her baby.

"Hey, you're a regular here," Martha said with a growl. "*You're* Viktor?"

"I am. I live close enough to walk here." He motioned toward where the beach lay just a couple of streets over. "And I'm guessing you're the best friend?"

"That's right," Martha growled.

Glen walked outside to see what had gotten his wife so upset and gave Viktor a curious look. "Hey man, good waves this morning?" Glen asked Viktor awkwardly.

"This is the vampire that impregnated Chastity," Martha snarled.

"Impregnated implies I took any part in the action," Viktor said with a frown. "My sperm was stolen."

Chastity looked at Glen for help. He put a hand on his wife and smiled at Viktor. "Coffee?"

"Can't turn down the best coffee in town," he said.

"It is," Chastity agreed. "I'd better get going, don't want to be late for the doctor."

Viktor looked down at his watch. "There's still time. Let me grab my coffee and I'll be right out. We might as well head together, since we're both here," he said and disappeared inside behind Glen before Chastity could respond.

"Well, that's interesting," Martha said, eyes locked on Viktor through the window.

"It's not. It's weird," Chastity insisted.

"He's hot, but I'll hate him if you want me to," Martha assured her like any dutiful best friend would. "Even though he's a regular who tips well."

Chastity just sipped her tea because she wasn't sure what she wanted from her friend. She'd felt defensive of Viktor when Martha was growling but she also didn't see why this all had to be easy on the man.

"Want my honest opinion?" Martha asked.

"No," Chastity said firmly then rolled her eyes. "Fine, give it to me."

"I think you should give the cutie a chance, but maybe it's just my hormones talking. I'm still raging through my second trimester," Martha laughed.

"You better go corner Glen before the lunch rush then," Chastity teased.

"I will, and here comes your sexy baby daddy so I suppose I'll talk to you later."

Martha walked back inside.

Viktor held the door for Martha, his eyes on her big belly as it swung by. His gaze swept to Chastity's flat stomach and she would have given anything to know what he was thinking. Probably envisioning how horrible she was going to look soon, all swelled and waddling.

"Want me to drive?" Viktor asked.

"I'm parked right here." Chastity motioned to her car and he agreed.

She didn't want the drive to the doctor's office to be awkwardly silent and she wasn't sure what to say to the man, so Chastity blared the nineties pop station, eliminating any potential need to talk. Viktor didn't complain and she even caught him mouthing the words to Britney Spears. She had to fake a cough to keep from laughing as his body did a little jerk every time he silently sang, *Hit me baby one more time.*

By the time she was parking she felt relaxed and even had a smile on her face. He wasn't awkward to be silent with and she liked that. Some people had to fill silence with inane chatter and some people made her feel like it was her job to do that. He was just there and comfortable.

When they walked into the clinic and she was handed a welcome packet and information sheets to fill out she started to get nervous again. This was supposed to be a single mother situation, now she had father information to fill out and she didn't even know the man's last name. It probably wasn't Lane, like Persia's.

"Do you want to fill out this part?" she finally asked after agonizing over it and wanting to pretend it wasn't there at all.

"Sure."

She watched him spell it out. Viktor Van Paulie.

That sent a shock through her. "Wait, is your dad Johnson Paulie? The bigshot vampire senator?" she gasped.

He cringed. "Yes, but please, don't judge me for what you see him do on TV."

"Oh, I wouldn't. You're obviously not a politician." She cringed a little, hoping that didn't sound as offensive to him as it did to her. "He's got some good ideas, though a bit extreme in some areas." She tried to sound convincing, but he looked at her like she'd missed the target there.

Johnson Paulie had run and lost for president multiple times since the vampires had come out of the coffin fifty years ago. He had been the vampire state representative for California for as long as Chastity could remember, which meant likely for all of Viktor's life. He believed in complete immersion of the species, which had gone great first in California and many other states had followed along. But he also believed that free feeding should be legal. Which meant biting and sipping from veins right out in the open. Right now it was treated as an okay thing to do behind closed doors with consent, sort of like sex. Everyone knew people did it, but in public no one wanted to see it.

Chastity couldn't help but shudder at the thought. She did not want to walk by a vampire sinking his fangs into some person, consensual or not. She looked at Viktor, her gaze drawn to his mouth which she knew hid retractable fangs. She wondered what he liked when feeding. She didn't know a lot about vampire feeding habits, but she had heard some vampires liked to play at attacking for their food, while others liked to have a human begging for it. Her body heated at both scenarios and she shifted uncomfortably in her seat.

"Ms. Martin," a nurse called, thankfully distracting her from the erotic turn of her thoughts.

Chastity needed to find out if vampire pregnancies were particularly horny affairs, because that would be something she'd need to prepare for. She took a deep breath and stood to follow the nurse. Viktor hesitated only a moment before standing to follow her as well. When he got close to the nurse, the woman startled, no doubt noticing his telltale eye color.

"Oh, friends should wait out here perhaps?" The nurse offered, giving Chastity an unsure look.

"I'm the father," Viktor mumbled at the same time Chastity said. "It's fine."

The nurse's eyes went wide but she just turned and led them back to an office. "Dr. Ricardo will meet you in his office first, he likes to talk things over before anyone gets naked," she laughed as if she'd said the same line a million times. She took Chastity's paperwork with a smile. "He'll be right in, have a seat."

"Maybe we should be seeing a vampire doctor," Viktor said as soon as they were seated.

"I'm not a vampire," Chastity scoffed. It hadn't even crossed her mind to go to anyone else. This was the doctor who worked with the clinic, she assumed he was reputable and that's all she'd needed. Now she wondered if Viktor was right, not that she'd admit it to him.

Viktor just looked meaningfully at her stomach and turned to study the man's desk which was clean and organized with just a few personality items like a mini sailboat and a picture of what she assumed was his family.

The doctor walked in, staring down at paperwork. He was older, probably near retirement age with grey hair and tan skin. He wore a white coat over a button up shirt with palm trees on it and khaki slacks. She had a feeling Viktor would suddenly approve of this choice of doctor and she now wanted to ask for anyone else.

"Well, Ms. Martin and Mr. Paulie, welcome and congratulations," he said, sitting and finally looking at them. He showed no surprise when he saw a human and vampire, probably because Viktor had marked off vampire as his species on the paperwork.

"Thank you," Chastity said.

"I am unfamiliar with hybrid babies, but I want to assure you right off that I am capable. I have seen women of all species through pregnancies and births. This is unusual but not an unprecedented scenario."

"But this *is* new to you," Viktor pointed out and Chastity was thankful, it wasn't enough that this doctor was confident.

Dr. Ricardo nodded. "Yes, and I understand you may have concerns, and while I plan to do some research about this particular situation, for now I will treat the pregnancy much the same as any other. Truly, women of all species carry children and birth much the same, so I don't see a problem. I will go ahead and take a look at everything today with an ultrasound. I wouldn't normally at this point in a pregnancy, but I think it's safest to peek at the implantation since the situation isn't ordinary."

He hesitated and Chastity's anxiety ramped up. She gripped the chair arms. A part of her wished Viktor would reach out and comfort her, but why would he? They weren't in a relationship, and he couldn't read her cues to know that she was in distress and needed comfort.

"The child should be fine though," Viktor prompted with a frown.

Dr. Ricardo gave a quick nod, "The child should be fine, there have been other instances of vampire-human matings. We won't really know what to expect as far as the fetus' needs for a while, depending on if it takes more of the vampire or human qualities, which is why we will schedule you for closer monitoring than I would usually recommend." He started typing some things on his computer. "I see from your clinic records that you were given a blood builder, how has that been going?"

Chastity thought about how she puked up everything she ate lately and frowned. "I have nothing to compare it to, but I am having morning sickness most of the day and find most food unappetizing."

Viktor glared at her.

"Well, keep taking them, they'll help. Morning sickness comes to all species, and you'll likely get out of the first trimester before feeling good again. Eat what you can, lots of water and fiber, fresh vegetables and fruits. Stay away from sugar and caffeine."

Chastity wrapped her arms around herself. Viktor was nodding with each order from the doctor and she felt attacked and alone.

"Well, follow me to the room where we'll do a quick exam, take some blood, and set up another appointment."

The doctor stood and walked to the door, holding it open for them. As she walked, she felt tears sting her eyes. All her dreams of this moment, none of them had included two men telling her what to eat and drink and suffer for the next three months.

They were led into an exam room where Chastity and Viktor were left alone.

"He seems alright," Viktor said.

Chastity shot her gaze to Viktor and scowled. "That's because you aren't the one puking ten times a day," she snapped.

Viktor's eyes widened but a nurse knocked and opened the door preventing a response.

The nurse had a bright smile for both of them but it didn't ease Chastity's nerves. "Hello, I'm Dr. Ricardo's nurse, Sandy. I need to take your vitals and some blood, then I'll have you undress just the bottom to prepare for the doctor's pelvic exam."

Chastity wanted to protest, she couldn't imagine letting that man anywhere near her pelvis. "I think this was a mistake," she said, panic in her voice.

"No doubt, but here we are," Viktor mumbled as Sandy attached a blood pressure cuff to her arm and shot a glare at the vampire.

"Dr. Ricardo is a very good doctor," Sandy assured Chastity. "It's normal to be nervous about your first child."

Chastity had no response. She wasn't sure if she was being hormonally ridiculous or not.

Viktor excused himself for the blood draw and so she could change. Once Sandy was done and Chastity was alone in the small cool room she debated making a run for it, but she couldn't pinpoint exactly what she was trying to run from.

Was it the reality of a child, or the fact that it was half vampire? Was it the thought of sharing this experience with Viktor, or was it really a problem with Dr. Ricardo? He had told her the blunt truth, she knew that morning sickness was common. She even knew that there wasn't much to be done but get through it. He wasn't telling her to suffer, he was being honest. Things would likely not get much better until the second trimester.

She took off her shorts and underwear then sat on the paper covered table and pulled a paper blanket over her lap. She could have called out for Viktor, but she didn't, she just sat in silence until there was another knock at the door.

In walked Viktor and Dr. Ricardo who had a softer look on his face than before. She wondered if the nurse had told him her blood pressure was high.

"Nervous?" he asked.

Chastity nodded.

"Well, your vitals look strong. I think you're handling things well so far despite your trouble keeping down food. The bloodwork will tell us if you are getting enough from the supplement the clinic gave you. A vampire fetus takes a lot more out of a mom than a human one. Even vampires take the stuff if they aren't regularly feeding from their mate for whatever reason."

Chastity relaxed, appreciating the explanation.

"Now, let's take a look down below."

Viktor scurried to stand by her head as she laid back and put her feet in the stirrups. He stared hard at the monitor, hands clasped in front of him as the doctor inserted a wand for a transvaginal ultrasound.

"It's early to hear a heartbeat, but what we are really after is making sure there's good attachment to the uterine wall and some obvious cell division," the doctor explained.

Black and grey filled the screen but when he paused and pointed out a small spot, Chastity bit her lip and felt tears prickle her eyes. That was her baby.

"What the hell am I looking at?" Viktor asked, ruining Chastity's moment.

"This is the egg sac, really all we have right now is a jumble of cells dividing like crazy. Another week or two and we'll hear the heartbeat, then things will start to take a more recognizable shape."

Viktor frowned and squinted at the screen. "Looks like a blob."

"Fuck you, that blob is my child," Chastity snapped, and he met her gaze with surprise and a bit of contrition.

Dr. Ricardo cleared his throat and removed the ultrasound wand. "Well, all looks as it should, I'll see you back in three weeks. We'll hear the heartbeat then, okay? In the meantime, call the office if you feel anything concerning. Take the blood builders, and when your bloodwork gets back I'll call if anything looks unusual. But I'd say we are looking at a normal healthy pregnancy. Congratulations."

With that, the doctor left, and Chastity started to cry.

CHAPTER TEN

Viktor didn't know what to do.

Chastity was laying on the table half covered with what looked like a giant paper towel and she was sobbing into her hands. Had she hoped the pregnancy wasn't going to be viable? Was she hoping she'd just be able to go try again and get what she had intended the first time?

"Want me to get the doctor back in here?" he asked. He'd warned the doctor before they came back in the room that Chastity was feeling very nervous about everything, and the man had seemed to understand and soften his tone with her, but Viktor still doubted she'd want to see more of the man. "Or nurse Sandy?"

"No," she sobbed.

"Do you want me to leave?"

"Yes," she said with a trembling voice that pulled at his protective instincts.

Viktor sighed and put a hand on her shoulder. "Hey, it's going to be alright."

"I know," she said with a hiccup.

"Were you hoping it wouldn't be?" He tried to keep accusation

COURTNEY DAVIS

out of his tone but judging by her stiffening he hadn't done a very good job.

"I am happy to have this child, half vampire or not," she said fiercely lowering her hands to meet his gaze. Her eyes were red rimmed and shining with tears, he hated the sight.

"So why the tears?" he finally asked in frustration.

"I don't know," she wailed, covering her face once again.

Viktor remembered his sister going through fits of emotions when she was pregnant, maybe that's all this was, and it meant there was not really anything he could do. "I'm going to step out so you can get dressed. Then do you want me to take you to lunch?"

She nodded, still covering her face.

Viktor walked to the door and turned to tell her that he'd see about any paperwork at the checkout desk. When he turned she had already started to move and the paper blanket fell away. His eyes locked onto her upper right inner thigh where a heart shaped strawberry birthmark was visible.

He sucked in a breath and hurried out of the room, leaning back against the door as his memory shifted back almost two years.

The woman was splayed out in a bronze bikini that shimmered in the sunlight. She didn't seem to notice or care that she was drawing attention from every creature on the beach and in the ocean. She was on her stomach, drawing in a sketchbook and completely sucked into what she was doing.

Viktor came out of the water and froze, his gaze devouring the beauty and when his eyes landed on a strawberry birthmark visible on her inner thigh his fangs descended.

"Shit," he scowled and hurried to the shop bathroom. He hadn't had a premature descension like that since he was in high school still drinking blood exclusively from bags.

By the time he had himself under control, having downed two blood bags while stroking his cock in the bathroom, he went back out ready to approach the vixen who had caused such a stimulating reaction.

But she was gone, and in his hurry to hide his embarrassment earlier, he'd never even gotten a look at her face. But he'd never forgotten that strawberry birthmark.

Viktor couldn't believe Chastity was his dream girl. His beach babe fantasy. How many times had he scanned the beach hoping to see a bronze bikini or a dark blonde haired beauty doodling in the sun.

Viktor steadied himself and headed to the checkout desk. He asked the secretary for any information she had on vampire-human pregnancies.

"Oh yeah, I know I saw some when I first started working here, but shit, I've never had to actually hand them out, let me look." She turned and started to dig around a drawer behind her as he signed a couple of forms.

A voice from behind sent a spike of dread through him.

"Viktor Paulie?"

Viktor turned stiffly and grimaced. "Treenly."

She hurried forward to give him a far too familiar embrace and cheek kiss. "I am shocked to run into you again so soon. First the art show and now here, of all places, it's as if the Gods are pushing us together."

Viktor didn't respond just snorted. If anything, this was the result of some kind of bad luck curse, wait, that would follow exactly why he was here in the first place. Fuck he hoped the Moon Goddess didn't intend him to have something to do with this bitch of a vampire too.

Treenly was unswayed by his lackluster response. "What the hell are you doing here? Is your sister pregnant again?"

"No," he said, trying not to panic. He wasn't ready for the

world to know about Chastity and he certainly didn't want Treenly to be the one to reveal it, and he knew she would if she could. She was a notorious gossip.

"Found them," the secretary said in triumph and passed him a couple of pamphlets.

Viktor grabbed them with a sharp *thank you* and shoved them in his pocket as fast as he could, praying to the Moon Goddess that Treenly hadn't caught the title. He said goodbye to Treenly, quick and rude, then rushed out the door feeling her narrowed gaze on him the whole way.

He walked to Chastity's car and waited. When Chastity came across the parking lot she had the same pamphlets in her hand. *The Vampire Human Pregnancy* scrawled across the front of them.

Fuck, he hoped Treenly hadn't spotted that.

"Are you doing okay?" he asked as she got close. Her eyes were still a little red, but she wasn't actively crying, that was an improvement.

"Yeah, I'm hungry though, and nauseous. Apparently, that's just my life for the next few months."

"If there was anything I could do to help, I would," he told her and she gave him a soft smile.

"Thank you, Viktor, I really appreciate that."

His heart fluttered a bit at her smile and words. He liked knowing that he'd done something right for her finally. He had to admit he hadn't exactly been his most charming since the first time they met. And if they were going to be doing this thing, this co-parenting thing, he knew that it would be best to have a friendly relationship. Which meant he needed to try harder.

"I know a great taco place if you think that sounds good," he offered as they got in the car.

"I love tacos usually, no promises I'll keep them down, but nothing sounds better," she admitted.

They ate tacos near the beach and read through the pamphlets together. They really didn't help ease Viktor's mind. They said that the fetus could have either a human or vampire appetite, and they wouldn't know for months. There was no most likely scenario, and there was nothing they could do to figure out things before they turned possibly deadly for both mother and child. The number of recorded human-vampire births was under a thousand worldwide and although many had been studied, there was still too little information to make Viktor comfortable.

By the time Chastity was dropping him off at home he was feeling even more conflicted.

"I don't like you being alone so much," he said, leaning in the open passenger door of her beetle.

"I'm fine, everything is fine," she assured him, not for the first time. "I am not about to change the fact that I live alone," she added with a sigh.

"Just ... call me if you need anything," he insisted.

She rolled her eyes. "I will."

Viktor closed the door and walked toward the beach. He had so many emotions about this whole thing and after seeing that blur that was his developing child, there was a new tug on something he hadn't thought he possessed. Now every time he looked at Chastity all he saw was how her being a human could be dangerous to his unborn child.

His phone rang and he frowned at his father's name.

"Hey Dad."

"What is this I hear about you being at an obstetrician's clinic with a human woman?"

Fuck, Viktor cursed silently and kicked at the sand. Treenly had wasted no time, she must have seen Chastity grab the pamphlets and put the obvious together. And since she'd been at Chastity's art show he wondered if she also recognized exactly *who* the human woman was. He hoped not.

"It's not something I'm ready to discuss with you," he said, keeping his tone neutral.

"I want to meet her, as soon as possible and I want this ...

incident controlled. Is she trying to shake you down for money? Child support? What's her end game here? Did you just have a one-night stand or did you two have a relationship? Are you sure it's even yours?"

Viktor wanted to snap and snarl at his father, wanted to defend Chastity, but he knew his father wasn't about to listen. Johnson Paulie had already made up his mind, all Viktor could do was keep him out of it for as long as possible.

"I'm not ready to discuss this with you. When I am, I'll call," he said and hung up.

His phone immediately rang again but Viktor ignored it. He sat in the sand and stared out at the water while the sun beat at his skin. He would need to cover up soon, he hadn't applied sunscreen since that morning. He held out until he could feel the burn before he got up and walked toward his shop and home. As he started up the stairs to his apartment his phone rang again, this time it was his sister.

"Hey," he said.

"Dad called to see if I knew anything about the human you're dating."

"Sorry, Treenly saw us at the clinic." He didn't have to elaborate, his sister knew exactly what kind of a vengeful gossip Treenly was.

CHAPTER ELEVEN

When Chastity got home she went right to her studio and started painting. Her stomach was holding down the tacos and she took advantage of the reprieve to create. She spent hours in the zone and when she stepped away, her thoughts coming back to the here and now, she realized the sun had set and she was starving.

She put a hand to her stomach and smiled, hungry was better than nauseous.

The next few weeks passed uneventfully. Viktor texted every day to check in but didn't show up at her house, which she appreciated. Or at least that's what she told herself.

She worked out a final design for Persia's project and judging by the woman's silence about the baby, she guessed Viktor hadn't told his sister. Maybe he was pretending that nothing was happening, maybe he was in denial?

But his daily texts said differently. She was on his mind. He wanted to know that she was doing alright, and it made her feel special.

The morning of her next appointment with Dr. Ricardo she headed into the city early to start on the mural.

Persia greeted her with hugs and squeals and snacks.

"Anything you need, *anything*, you just let me know," Persia said and grinned so wide Chastity saw the tips of her retracted fangs.

"I'm okay. I'll just do a bit of sketching today, outline things and then tomorrow I'll lay down some serious paint. I have an appointment this afternoon otherwise I could easily stay all day. I have a hard time stopping when I'm in a creative zone."

Persia gave her another wide grin then left her to it and Chastity soon found herself content in the creative process. She stopped halfway through the sketching to sip at the juice Persia had brought her. Unfortunately, it wasn't orange juice like she'd suspected, it was something with pineapple. A flavor she didn't enjoy on a good day but battling morning sickness, she was running for the bushes and emptying her stomach almost immediately after a sip.

"Gross, I play there!" a beautiful little girl said as she stood nearby with a look of disgust on her face.

"Sorry," Chastity said as she wiped her face on the hem of her shirt. She looked at the child that had to be Persia's daughter, Viktor's niece, and wondered how much her own child would look like this. The red-brown eyes and the golden blonde hair so much like Viktor's. She was paler than Viktor, more the tone of most vampires. Her lips were ruby red, and Chastity wondered if the child had just fed.

She shuddered at the thought and bent to unload the rest of her stomach's contents.

"Oh no!" Persia yelled and rushed over, rubbing her back. "Oh dear, Lacey go get Chastity some water and a wet towel."

Persia led her to a seat and Chastity was thankful for both the water and wet towel delivered by a scowling little girl.

"Sorry about that, I'll clean it up in a minute."

"Oh, don't worry about that, I'll send the housekeeper out with a hose. I puked every day for six months when I was pregnant with Lacey, I get it."

"Oh …" Chastity said, unsure if she should admit that's exactly what her problem was.

"It's okay. I know," Persia whispered.

"You do?"

"Yeah, Viktor told me the day you were both here."

"Does anyone else know?"

"Well, you two were spotted at the clinic, so our father has been notified of the possibilities, but thankfully he hasn't been able to threaten your name or any details out of Viktor yet."

"I'm not sure how I feel about all that," she admitted.

"Understandable. This is an unusual situation for both of you. I just hope you realize that Viktor's a good guy. I hope you also know, now that you know that I know, that you can call me if you need anything or have any questions. Or if you just want to talk about swollen ankles and pregnancy cravings."

Chastity smiled weakly at Persia, feeling genuine warmth from the woman. "Thank you."

"And if you want to complain about my doofus of a brother, you can call me too, I have all the dirt," she said with a wink.

Chastity laughed then, and felt better about a lot of things after that conversation. She worked on the mural for a couple more hours then rushed to her appointment.

When she entered the waiting room, Viktor was already there, reading a parenting magazine.

"I already checked us in," he said.

"Thanks," she said, unsure of how she felt about him taking control like that. She sat in the seat next to him mostly because the only other open seat was across the room and it would have seemed rude to sit where they couldn't possibly hold a conversation.

"How is my sister's mural coming along?"

She shouldn't be surprised he knew she'd been there, they probably talked about her. "I puked in her bushes."

Viktor laughed and she liked the way it sounded. She also liked the way it lit up his face. All the strong lines of his features softened with his mirth and it was a look that would have melted the panties right off of her if they were on a date.

She wiggled slightly in her seat as her body started to react with desire. She really needed to find out if vampire pregnancies were particularly horny affairs.

"Are you okay, Chastity?" Viktor asked, his voice low and his eyes dark.

Chastity froze and looked at him. Could he tell how her body was betraying her right now? And shit, those eyes and that low voice were not doing anything to ease it up.

"I—" The nurse called her name then and she jumped up, eager to put some space between herself and Viktor.

"Right this way, and you must be Mr. Martin?" the nurse asked as Viktor followed behind her.

"Mr. Paulie," Viktor corrected and the nurse didn't even blink an eye just showed them back to an exam room.

"How have things been going for you, Ms. Martin?"

"About the same, still sick most of the time. I'm just trying to find what triggers it and avoid those things."

The nurse made a sympathetic sound as she wrapped Chastity's arm in a blood pressure cuff. "Any other worries you're having today?"

Chastity almost scoffed at the question, she was nothing *but* worries, however she wasn't going to share that, she might find herself under psychological care if she admitted that. "I don't think so, just anxious to hear that everything is growing like it should be."

"Well, the doctor will be right in to check that for you, no need to undress today."

Chastity nodded as the nurse left and then it was just her and

Viktor in a tiny room. She couldn't look at him, she stared at the diagrams of dilation on the wall as if she were studying for an exam. She could feel Viktor observing her but he didn't speak and she was thankful.

When the door opened and Dr. Ricardo walked in wearing a bright shirt with wiener dogs on surf boards under his white coat, she was actually glad to see him.

"How are you doing today, Chastity?" he asked brightly and she repeated the answer she'd given the nurse.

"That is normal, and your vitals look great. Let's take a closer look at the bundle of joy."

Chastity was thankful to not be asked to undress for this appointment. It was an outer ultrasound so she just laid back, lifted her shirt, and pushed her stretchy shorts down. She bit her lip as she stared at Viktor who seemed transfixed by the exposed skin. Was he disgusted with her body? Did he think that she was too tan? For a human she was considered a little on the pale side with freckles on a good portion of her body but compared to a vampire she had a definite golden glow.

Dr. Ricardo started to prod and push at her abdomen, distracting her from her worries.

"What are you doing?" Viktor demanded, his voice cold.

"Don't worry I am not hurting her or the baby, I am just feeling for the top of the uterus. As the pregnancy progresses, so will the position of her uterus. Everything looks good on the outside," he assured them both.

Viktor continued to watch everything Dr. Ricardo did with a serious set to his lips. Chastity was comforted by Viktor's vigilance.

When the ultrasound began, a heartbeat was suddenly pulsing around the room.

"It's so fast," Chastity whispered.

"Vampire heartbeats are fast, but so are fetus' so it's not really telling at this point," Dr. Ricardo said. Then he continued moving the wand around, revealing a shape he claimed was a baby but looked more like an alien blob to Chastity. He measured things declaring they were all perfect, which made her smile and Viktor let out a sigh of relief

They left with orders to keep up the good work and return in three weeks.

Viktor walked Chastity to her car, his mind holding on to the image of her exposed skin. She was a delicate shade because she spent much of her time inside a studio, painting. He liked it, the cream of her skin and the spattering of freckles he'd seen on her belly. Ones he'd immediately wanted to follow with his finger, and then his tongue.

He cleared his throat as they reached their cars and hesitated, he needed to keep his mind off of her body and the things he wanted to do to it. What better way than bringing up his father. "My father wants to meet you."

Chastity raised an eyebrow and crossed her arms over her chest. "Do *you* want me to meet your father?"

Viktor ran a hand through his hair. The short answer was no, of course not, his father was a controlling asshole. But the reality was that it would need to happen eventually so why put it off?

"He's in town next week, it would be a convenient time to do introductions. We could do dinner at my sister's house, she already offered it as neutral ground. If you're not comfortable though, we don't have to."

Chastity twisted her lips and looked thoughtful. "I suppose it makes sense seeing as everything is growing well. So why don't you come to dinner at my house tomorrow night and you can meet *my* father. If we aren't avoiding the meet the family thing forever, let's get it over with."

Viktor was pleased with the invitation. He'd spent the last few weeks trying to give her space but he'd wanted to drive to her house every day and see with his own eyes that she was alright. He had also been walking to Mooncalled Coffee daily hoping to run into her and he was pretty sure Martha had figured him out because she gave him a knowing smirk every time he walked in the door.

"Is there anything I can bring?" he asked.

"Maybe bring your own refreshment?" she said with a nervous smile.

"Of course, I would never expect you to provide blood bags for me but is there anything else? Dessert perhaps?"

She grinned and the sight of the smile lighting up her face made his stomach flutter; he wanted to see a lot more of those.

"That would be great, no pineapple," she added.

"I wouldn't dream of it," he assured her. "Anything else you're avoiding?"

"Nothing that you'd put in a dessert," she assured him with a laugh. "Thanks for checking."

"Of course, I want to do whatever I can to make things easier for you through this. I know we didn't plan this together, but I hope you realize I am here for whatever you need." He didn't add that he wanted to be even closer for those needs too, but the thought did filter through his mind.

"Thank you, Viktor," Chastity said, then leaned close and lifted tall to place a quick kiss on his cheek before getting in her car.

Viktor stepped away so she could pull out and although the kiss was the sort of thing his own sister planted on him whenever she saw him, it felt like so much more. Heat from his cheek raced through his head making him feel light.

Viktor drove home with his fangs slightly descended and a goofy grin on his face.

He sent a text to his sister and father about dinner plans. Persia responded with a heart emoji and a thumbs up, his father sent an ominous, *Acceptable.*

CHAPTER TWELVE

Chastity was nervous. She'd spent the morning painting at Persia's house where the woman had chattered on and on about the coming dinner she planned. She asked for Chastity's input on all the dishes to be served, which Chastity thought was nice but eventually it started to make her nervous. It sounded like more than a dinner to meet Viktor's father, it sounded like an event.

Then Chastity had hurried home to shower and cook for her own little dinner for three. It was going to be a far simpler affair, and she only felt a little anxious about that. Would Viktor see her simple life as a lack? His family wasn't much larger—he had just the one sibling—but they were wealthy, and apparently served four course meals regularly.

But it didn't matter. She wouldn't let it matter. She was making a pot roast, rare because that's what her father preferred and she knew vampires ate meat as red as possible. She'd also make a salad and she'd picked up some rolls. It was simple, but so was she. She didn't need more and if Viktor did, well this wasn't a date so who the hell cared?

At least that is what she kept trying to tell herself as she fretted over every detail.

She put on a blue and white summer dress, braided her hair, and applied a little makeup. She stared at herself in the mirror, turning this way and that, trying to decide if she was showing yet.

She wasn't, but she certainly *felt* pregnant; hungry and nauseous.

When the doorbell rang and she heard her father let himself in she relaxed. He always made everything okay.

"Chastity!" he called out, "I found a handsome vampire standing by the house, is he yours?"

Chastity's face flamed. Her father also tended to say things that mortified her.

"Only if his name is Viktor and he looks like he just jumped off a surfboard," she called back.

When she walked to the entryway she saw that it was indeed Viktor with her father, but he wasn't dressed for the beach today. She was shocked to see him in dark jeans and a black t-shirt looking more like he was heading to the bar than the beach. It sent a little thrill up her spine and had her wondering if she was already hitting that second trimester horniness? She'd looked it up, vampires don't have hornier pregnancies than humans.

Next to Viktor stood her father with the same grin on his face he'd had since she was a child. His short silver hair was gelled back and he was wearing khaki slacks and a blue button up with pearl buttons. It was a little more than his usual casual dinner look and she wondered if he was nervous about meeting Viktor tonight.

"Hey, I'm glad you two met already, and I hope you're both hungry." She gave her father a quick kiss on the cheek and turned to Viktor, not sure how to greet the man who was the father of her baby, but also they'd never been intimate and technically knew each other for less time than she'd been pregnant with his child. A kiss was definitely too much, and a handshake seemed ridiculous so she just stood there feeling awkward.

"Dessert," Viktor said, handing her a pie and thankfully taking the greeting decision away from her. "It's cherry. I haven't heard that it's on your *do not eat* list yet," he said with a grin.

Chastity warmed knowing he cared. "Not yet. Let's hope it stays that way."

Chastity hurried to the kitchen.

"Her mother puked every day for nine months," her dad said to Viktor as they followed, "but she still managed to grow a healthy girl of seven and a half pounds so I wouldn't worry about it."

"I don't like knowing she's ill," Viktor said. "I know my sister struggled the first months of pregnancy, but it should end, right?"

Chastity touched her stomach, "Maybe I'll find joy in the second trimester."

"I've heard that," Viktor mumbled, and Chastity's cheeks burned. She was thankful her father had wandered into the living room to look at some of her new paintings lined up on the wall and had missed that last remark.

Chastity busied herself pulling out food and setting it on the table. She heard the low rumble of both men's voices in the living room. She knew her father was an easy man to talk to so it didn't surprise her, but she *was* surprised at how it pleased her to hear them getting along. She didn't dare hope that she would have the same easy repartee with Viktor's father. What would she even talk to a senator about?

Dinner was ready so she poured a sparkling water for herself and called them to the table.

"You've been busy," her father said as he sat in his usual spot at the head of the small table. Chastity sat to his right putting her in easy access to the kitchen, her usual spot, and Viktor sat at the other end of the table to her right. It was cozy, but it was all she'd ever needed. She imagined a highchair across from her in front of the large kitchen window and it was a pleasant thought. This could possibly be a regular thing, the three of them plus a baby.

Or would that be weird once the baby came and her and Viktor weren't in a relationship? Would he ever want to join them for dinner? She supposed not and that dampened her joy a bit.

"Are you feeling ill?" Viktor asked.

"Oh, yeah, I think I'm just hungry," she said.

"She forgets to eat when she's working, her mother was the same way with her sculpting."

Viktor frowned at her and Chastity wanted to kick her father under the table for outing her like that. Viktor didn't need more reason to think she wasn't taking care of herself.

Her dad quickly changed the subject. He asked Viktor about his business and family, and Viktor answered in detail. Chastity was surprised to learn Viktor was quite successful and busy with his surf instructions and running the shop and rental business. It was way more than a hobby that paid for itself, and he invested in a line of sunscreen for vampires that was still in a testing phase as well as a line of surf shorts he helped his friend design.

He was more than a trust fund beach bum.

She wondered how his father felt about all that he'd accomplished. She'd always heard the senator's son mentioned as a millionaire playboy disappointment; gaining sympathy for the senator from voters who were similarly disappointed in the paths their children had taken. Sort of a *we are all the same, even if I do drink blood*, sort of ploy. Maybe it *was* just a ploy, because Viktor was not what she would have expected that mentioned son to be. His father was probably actually proud of him.

"I understand this is a situation neither of you expected," her dad said as Chastity served pie. "But I am glad to see you two getting along, the child will benefit greatly from having you both, I'm sure."

"I always expected to be a part of a child's life," Viktor pointed out. "It's probably less weird for me than it is for Chastity.

Vampires often have children without a relationship because fertility issues are so rampant among our species."

"And you have no others?" her father pressed.

"No sir, this will be my first, possibly only. I didn't imagine having a large family ever."

That was a surprise to Chastity. She looked up and met his gaze. Had she been given his only child? At least it wasn't her fault, and obviously he could give another sample at any point if he wanted a child that was fully vampire, though she'd be surprised if he ever trusted that process again. Maybe he'd try the natural way.

Why did she hope he didn't do either?

"That means you'll have lots of time for this one," her father said brightly. "Being a father has been the best thing in my life." He squeezed Chastity's shoulder. "I only had one and because she was perfect, that was enough."

Chastity rolled her eyes at the familiar line. She knew that the reality was that her parents had met when they were older and so there'd been only enough time for one child.

"What about you, Chastity? Do you plan to have more?" Viktor asked her.

Chastity shook her head. "I hadn't thought about anything past this one, honestly. At my age, I'm not sure more than one would be a good idea and it was a rather expensive process."

"You could though," Viktor insisted. "You could meet someone, get married, and have a child the old-fashioned way."

"So could you," she shot back, uncomfortable with the line of questioning.

Viktor nodded and they ate pie silently.

After pie and a little more conversation mostly upheld by her father who was never short on words, Chastity walked her father out onto the porch as Viktor cleared the table. "Thanks for coming," she said, hugging him tightly.

"Any time and hey, he seems like a nice guy. I know this isn't what you expected but sometimes life chooses for us."

"Sometimes *chaos* chooses for us," she agreed.

"Call me tomorrow," he laughed and walked off toward his car.

Chastity went back inside and found Viktor had gotten half the dishes done already. "You don't need to do that."

He didn't turn to look at her. "You cooked, I should clean."

Chastity wasn't going to argue with that, she hated doing the dishes. She sat on a stool and watched him as he worked, quick and efficient. His shirt was tight, unlike the tropical ones he usually wore. His lean muscles bulged and moved as he washed and dried at the sink. Chastity started to fantasize what those muscles would look like moving on top of her, under her, between her legs ...

She must have made a noise because he turned suddenly and she didn't have time to hide the desire that was showing on her face.

"Chastity?" he asked quietly.

She shook her body and stood up. "Well thanks for coming over," she said, her voice husky.

He looked like he wanted to say something but decided against it and dried off his hands even though the dishes weren't quite done. She followed him to the door where he hesitated. He turned to her and his eyes bored into hers as if they were searching for an answer to the question her body had asked in the kitchen.

Part of her wanted him to lean down and kiss her, but a more reasonable part of her knew that it would be an unnecessary complication.

"If you need *anything*, call me," he said, his voice low.

She had to tighten every muscle in her body to keep from visibly shivering at the sound. "Okay," she managed and bit her lip.

"If you weren't already pregnant with my kid, I think I'd ask you out on a date," he said with a smooth smile.

His words burned all the desire from her, and she took a step back, scowled, and grunted. "Sure, ruined goods now, huh. See you at dinner next week," she snapped and walked away from the still open door.

She heard him curse, then the door shut, and she knew he was gone. She walked straight to her bed and flopped onto it.

What an asshole!

Viktor cursed himself as he walked to his van. Everything had been going so well, too well maybe, and he'd had to fuck it up with that comment. Of course it was offensive, he'd heard the way it sounded as soon as it came out of his mouth. And it hadn't even been true. He didn't give a fuck if she was pregnant with his kid, or anyone else's, he'd love to take her out on a date.

Maybe that's why he had said it. He was scared of how much he wanted her.

He hadn't felt this drawn to a woman beyond the possibility of a sexual encounter in years. The only real relationship he'd ever had was when he was in his early twenties. He'd been freshly free from his father's grasp and starting his business when he'd met Farah. She was a vampire woman a little older than himself and they'd had a lot of fun together. He'd fallen in love with her and started to see a future together. Unfortunately, she'd only been looking for a good time and when she'd decided it was time to look at settling down, he hadn't been the option for her. She'd chosen a man who was older and well established in a career, and it had broken his young heart.

He'd never dated anyone seriously since and his heart had remained intact.

Until now, because that child growing inside of Chastity would hold a piece forever, he knew and expected that. But its mother, could she end up with a piece too? He was terrified to say yes, it was far too dangerous a feeling for him to have because when Chastity inevitably chose some human man to be her partner for life, she'd leave him in the cold where he would shatter along with any part of his heart he'd given her.

He had to stay separate, she was a parenting partner, that was all, that was safe.

CHAPTER THIRTEEN

Two days before she was supposed to meet Viktor's father at dinner, Chastity was sitting outside Mooncalled, sipping tea and staring down a banana bran muffin.

"He actually said that? And you didn't punch him in the nuts?" Martha growled.

Chastity laughed at her friend's disappointment. "No, but I walked away and didn't even give him the satisfaction of a slammed door in his face. I have also ignored his texts. The only reason I relented on that today is he threatened to come check on me. The last thing I want is for him to be in my space right now."

"Because you're worried you'll try to suck his dick?"

"Martha," Chastity gasped, but she couldn't hide her grin as she forced a bite of muffin into her mouth.

Martha just laughed. "You know it's really unfair that you're going to have his kid but you didn't get a taste of that delicious body. Perhaps you should try him out. I mean, you're already not having an anonymous pregnancy, so you might as well go back and get the good stuff."

Chastity shook her head at her horny friend, she couldn't even say she hadn't thought the same thing. The problem was she

HAVING THE VAMPIRE'S BABY

hadn't ever slept with a vampire before and she didn't entirely know what to expect. "I don't want to complicate things more," she said. It was a half-truth.

"I get it, if you guys can keep things friendly it'll be good for the kid."

"Exactly." But it left her wanting. "Maybe you can introduce me to one of Glen's cousins or something."

"Yeah, I'm sure at least one of them has a pregnancy kink."

"Ugh," Chastity sighed and laid her head on the table. "I'm doomed until I have the baby and get my body back in order, aren't I?"

Martha shrugged, "Maybe, maybe not," she said slyly.

Chastity pulled her head up and gave her friend a distrustful eye. Martha was looking across the street and Chastity followed her gaze to a vampire dressed in wet board shorts and an unbuttoned tropical shirt. His hair was messy and half wet like he'd just run out of the ocean. He probably had.

Viktor hurried across the street and stopped at the table, his eyes running up and down Chastity like he was assessing the most important of documents. "You look well," he said with relief.

"I am," she agreed, trying to keep her gaze off his exposed chest. He had a sparse amount of hair on it, just enough for her gaze to follow all the way down to his low-rise waistband.

"I'll get your usual," Martha said, leaving the two alone.

Viktor took Martha's vacated seat. "Are you going to the fest tomorrow?"

The Beach Fest was a summer tradition for their oceanside town. A one-night carnival with food and fun right on the main beach and it was usually a wild time, especially after most of the families left and the stands started overserving alcohol. She had always gone and had a fun time too. She hadn't thought much about going this year though.

"I'm not sure, I've been pretty tired lately," she admitted.

101

He nodded. "That's normal?" he asked.

"I suppose it is. My body is making an entire being at the moment," she said, giving her flat belly a rub.

He seemed at a loss for words, staring at where she rubbed her stomach through her t-shirt. He cleared his throat and met her gaze, his was heavy in a way she wasn't sure she understood. "And how is that going?" he asked, his voice a little rough.

Was she imagining things, or did he seem a little distracted by her body? "Good, I think. I'm dealing at least. Working a lot too, which helps keep my mind off of everything."

Viktor frowned. "Are you eating enough? You should be resting if you're tired."

"Right ... and I would pay the bills with what exactly, if I rested all day?" she asked.

Martha arrived then with a cup for Viktor. "Cinnamon latte, iced for the vampire," she said.

"Thank you," Viktor said.

"Martha is way more pregnant than me and works almost every day," Chastity glared.

"Uh oh," Martha said as she accepted Viktor's cash. "What did you say?"

"I merely suggested she take it easy while she's feeling so tired and ill with the pregnancy," Viktor defended.

Martha huffed a laugh. "Chastity paints, it's not like she's hauling boxes or running marathons."

Now Chastity turned her glare on Martha. Sure, her work wasn't physically taxing, other than standing for long periods of time maybe, but it's not like just anyone could do it.

Martha held up her hands and scurried away, obviously seeing the fight in her friend's eyes.

"I suppose you're fine, but I don't see you every day so I can't judge how well you're taking care of yourself," Viktor reasoned.

A part of her knew he was being reasonable, but a bigger part of her was still hurt by his words and that part refused to listen to his advice.

"I didn't choose you; I didn't want a partner in this, Viktor, so back off," she said and left the table.

Viktor watched her go with his mouth hanging open. What the hell had just happened? He had planned to be calm and nice. He'd planned to make a reasonable request to know how she was doing, but she got him so confused. Her body tempted him and that made him mad, then she refused to be reasonable about taking care of herself and that made him even more mad. So of course he said things that pissed her off.

Martha came back out and took Chastity's empty seat. "Listen, I am on your side," she said.

That took Viktor by surprise and he lifted an eyebrow at Martha to urge her to continue.

"She works hard, she forgets to eat, and she feels shitty all day. She's trying to be tough, but I worry about her. She doesn't know what's normal for a human pregnancy, let alone a half-vampire one. I am sure she needs something more, unfortunately I'm only an expert on werewolf pregnancies."

Viktor turned his eyes in the direction Chastity had disappeared. He knew Martha was right, but that didn't mean Chastity was going to change her feelings about getting advice from him.

"Thanks, I need to go," he said and hurried home, then jumped in his van.

Chastity may not like it, but he was a part of this and if she wouldn't take care of herself, he'd do it for her. He ran to the store and gathered everything he thought he needed, then drove to her house before he could think better of his plan of invasion.

As he hauled the groceries up her walkway, he waved at the neighbor who wasn't even trying to pretend she wasn't watching what he was doing. The woman waved back but didn't smile, just watched him and he hoped her curiosity extended to Chastity's well-being and not just gossip.

He knocked firmly on Chastity's door. He waited but no answer came, he knocked again.

"She doesn't hear a damn thing when she's in her studio," the neighbor called out helpfully.

Viktor grunted a thank you, not sure if the neighbor would have told any stranger that information or if she'd recognized him. Either way, he was going to have to talk to Chastity about locking her front door because when he tried it, it opened right up.

He let himself in, took the groceries to the kitchen and frowned down at the half-eaten breakfast sitting on the counter and the empty bottle of blood builder pills. How long ago had she run out?

He pulled out his phone and sent off a quick text then went to her studio. She'd pointed out the door when he'd come for dinner, but she hadn't let him in. It was her private space; he understood her hesitancy.

He stood undecided at the door for a minute. He could hear a quiet hum of music inside so he was certain she was there. Was she going to be pissed that he was invading her privacy? Probably. Was he right to be there though? Yes, he thought so. She was pregnant with his child and therefore he had a vested interest in her health and well-being. He had a right and a responsibility even to make sure that the baby grew healthy. And right now, the only way to do that, was to make sure Chastity was taken care of too.

He pushed the door open, calling her name softly.

She screamed, spun, and threw a wet paintbrush in his direction.

Viktor frowned down at the splotches of red on his shirt and shorts.

"What the fuck, Viktor?" she snapped. "You scared the shit out of me."

"You didn't answer the door, and your neighbor said you don't hear anything when you're in your studio. She basically told me to walk in uninvited. Does she want you to get murdered?"

"Mrs. Layton is a nosy bitch, she likely recognized you." Chastity's eyes were blazing and her cheeks were flushed with anger.

She was beautiful and he couldn't help smiling at her even as she crossed her arms over her chest and stared at him with contempt. She was definitely pissed, but he wasn't sure if it was because he was at her house, or because he'd snuck up on her. Something about it all made him want to laugh and kiss her.

The thought took him so off guard he stepped back. "I brought food. I will cook you something for an early dinner or late lunch … breakfast maybe? I saw the kitchen, when's the last time you ate a full meal and when did you run out of pills?" He latched onto all the things he was worried about and ignored the desires that were creeping in on him.

"Breakfast didn't sit well, that's why I was at the coffee shop. Muffins and tea sometimes are all I can handle," she admitted.

And he'd scared her away from it. Viktor cursed himself. "And the pills?" he prompted, trying to keep his mind on track. He was here to assess how well she was taking care of herself and help where he could.

"A couple of days ago. I just didn't want to leave the house to get more."

"Why didn't you call me? I could have brought some. I could have brought food too," he said softly.

"Why would I do that? You don't owe me. You aren't my boyfriend." The last statement was said with a touch of sadness that tugged at his heart.

"Chastity, I care about you." He took a step toward her,

wondering if she'd welcome a hug from him. When she didn't move away he put his arms around her in a light embrace. He was instantly inundated with her scent, it filled his nostrils and went straight to his groin. His fangs started to descend and he was desperate to stop the reaction before he really embarrassed himself. "I care because you are pregnant with my child," he said, mostly to remind himself why he was there.

She pushed out of his embrace and narrowed her eyes at him. "Right."

He took a deep breath and ignored the disappointment at the loss of her body heat. "Look, we are in this together. I want to help, so please, let me help."

She looked like she was about to tell him to fuck off but then she grabbed a rag and held it out to him. "You should wipe off the paint before it dries, you're lucky I was using water-based today. I only use oil-based outside now, even though this studio is well ventilated."

He took the rag and wiped at his shirt but didn't really care if it was ruined. She was accepting his offer of help, and that made his heart flutter and a knot eased in his stomach. "I'll go wash up and start cooking."

"Okay," she agreed and if he wasn't mistaken, he thought he saw a hint of relief on her face.

Had she just been waiting for someone to come in and demand to take care of her? Because if she needed a firm hand, he'd be happy to offer. His cock hardened as he walked to the bathroom and images of taking control of her filled his mind. *Fuck*, he needed to keep his mind out of the bedroom. She was pregnant with his baby; he couldn't risk making their relationship awkward with sex, and besides, she hadn't given him any signals that she'd be interested in pursuing something physical with him.

CHAPTER FOURTEEN

Chastity stared at the door after it closed behind Viktor. What the hell was that? And why did it make her feel so content? She'd never been the type to want or need someone to take care of her, but knowing he'd come here to do just that was making her feel warm. That hug had been amazing too, until he'd opened his big dumb mouth again.

She shook her head and gave herself a firm talk down. He was trying to boss her around and control her just because he had a claim on the baby she was making. This had nothing to do with him feeling things for her outside of that.

She had to remember that's all it was, because her libido wanted to argue that it was all about her own sexy body and personality. Her libido wanted her to jump on the poor guy and ravage him when all he was trying to do was make her eat so the baby could grow properly.

She took her time closing up paints and washing her hands in the studio sink, then she hung up her apron and went into the house. She paused after quietly shutting the studio door. The sounds of someone cooking in her kitchen felt odd. No one had ever cooked for her here. Her father had helped her a couple of times, but this was different, this felt … domestic.

She walked toward the kitchen, the smells that were wafting out made her groan and her stomach rumbled. "What are you making?"

He turned and smiled at her. "Steak and eggs, I think you need the protein and the blood, sorry, you're getting rare."

She didn't argue, just sat at the table where a couple of glasses and a bottle of orange juice sat. She poured a glass and sipped as she watched him move around her kitchen. She wasn't sure how to handle being taken care of. Part of her wanted to jump up and help, part of her wanted to tell him to let her do it for him, and a part of her wanted to soak up the attention because she knew she deserved it and wasn't sure when she'd get it again.

When he finished and turned with a smile, she felt her heart lurch a little. He set two plates on the table and she thanked him quietly, not trusting her voice to not betray the emotions she was feeling.

Her mouth watered as she looked at the meal and she wanted to eat with enthusiasm but she went slow, expecting to have to stop due to nausea like usual. But it never came. She ended up eating everything on her plate and even felt tempted to lick the damn thing of its bloody meat juices.

It wasn't until she was done that she noticed Viktor was barely eating his own food but had apparently been distracted by watching her with intense eyes and a satisfied sort of smirk on his face.

Her cheeks heated with embarrassment. "Oh my god, I haven't eaten that much … ever maybe," she said with a laugh. "I don't know what you did to it, but damn."

His self-satisfied smile widened. "I added a synthetic blood supplement as a seasoning." He pushed his plate toward her then got up and grabbed a bottle off the counter. "Eat that, I'm not as hungry as you," he said with a wink. "Vampires use this seasoning in a lot of cooking. It gives food an extra kick and adds some needed sustenance that regular food doesn't give us since we mostly eat for pleasure, not nutrition."

Of course, why hadn't she looked into other ways to get vampire nutrition? She suddenly felt like an idiot and completely incapable of taking care of her child, her half vampire child.

She burst into tears.

"What?" Viktor hissed then hurried around the table and pulled her up and into his arms.

Chastity clung to his shirt and sobbed against his chest. Damn he smelled good. His hands stroked up and down her back soothingly until her sobs were only hiccups of embarrassment and shame.

"I don't even know how to take care of my own child," she whispered against his chest. "What the hell am I doing?"

Viktor pulled back and forced eye contact, she saw no judgment there and it eased most of her embarrassment.

"Hey, no, you're doing fine, Chastity. This would be overwhelming for anyone and it's certainly new to me, too."

"Sure, but it's still why you're here isn't it? Because you think I'm incapable of taking care of myself? Because I have no idea what a vampire needs, so how can I possibly care for a helpless baby one."

"That's not completely true," he said carefully.

When she tried to wiggle out of his embrace, he tightened it.

"Listen. You didn't do this on purpose, you were tricked, same as me. Now we are learning how to deal. Let me help you, Chastity. Let me be here and take care of you and the baby while you're learning how to deal with this half-vampire fetus thing. No one would expect you to know what to do, and no one is judging you for trying to figure it out. But it will be easier if you let me help."

With each plea to let him help her she relaxed and warmed, and her heart fluttered. She wasn't alone and she hadn't realized just how much she'd needed to feel that.

"Okay," she whispered on a shaky breath.

His arms loosened and she leaned back, wiping snot and tears off of his shirt. "Sorry about that."

"No worries, I think you already ruined it with paint anyway."

She looked up at him ready to defend herself, he had broken into her house after all. But he was smiling, and his eyes were bright with mirth.

"Maybe knock next time," she pointed out.

Their gazes locked and then his eyes shifted briefly, and she was certain he glanced at her mouth. Was he going to kiss her? Did she want him to?

She licked her lips in anticipation, and he stiffened.

A knock at the front door broke the spell and he released her so fast she had to use the table to keep herself straight.

"That would be a delivery," he explained and hurried to the door.

Chastity tried to calm her racing heart and fired up libido as she cleared the table, not able to resist taking a couple bites of what he hadn't eaten. When Viktor returned, he handed her a bottle of blood builder pills.

"I'll happily get some for you when you are low so you don't have to leave your work to go to the store and you don't run out completely."

It didn't sound like chastisement, but Chastity still stiffened in defense because she knew she should have made time to go get more. "Thanks."

He nodded. "I better get back to the shop, but if it's alright, I'll call and check on you tonight. It won't be until later though; I have lessons to teach after sunset."

She nodded. "Sure, of course," she said and popped the bottle, taking a pill to distract herself from the disappointment of him leaving.

"I'll pick you up for the carnival tomorrow night. Take a nap this afternoon and eat a good dinner," he ordered as he left the house.

When she heard the front door close behind him, she sat back at the table and finished off his steak as she tried to make sense of her confusing feelings.

Did she like Viktor? Or was she just horny because of pregnancy?

Or was she so starved for attention and being taken care of that she was willing to sell her body for a little care? None of her ex-boyfriends had been particularly good at caretaking. She'd dated one who liked to cook, but he only made what he liked and never asked her what she wanted. She'd dated a guy briefly that called her constantly, but only to ask her what color her underwear was and if she could send him a picture of it.

This was a new experience for her, and she liked it far too much considering he wasn't her boyfriend at all.

She needed to remember that this wasn't a normal dating situation, in fact not a dating situation at all. She needed to make sure she didn't do anything to make their already complicated relationship more so. He would be in her life forever because of the child, no reason to make that awkward.

And if she let her mind drift toward some kind of daydream about him wanting her, she reminded herself that he had never planned on having a full-time child. He had always wanted to raise a child with another couple, to be a part-time dad. He'd never be interested in her seriously with the full dad responsibility on him.

Not that she needed him to be interested in her, or be a full-time father for her unborn child. That hadn't ever been her plan either.

If only her libido would catch up to that fact because right now it kept telling her she should see what he looked like naked and reminding her of how sweet it was that he had taken care of her this afternoon.

"Shit," she snapped at herself then stood up to clean the dishes. She'd need to keep herself well distracted, and maybe pull out her vibrator too.

CHAPTER FIFTEEN

The next evening she was feeling better than she had in weeks. She wasn't sure if it was the blood builder vitamins she was back on, or the seasoning Viktor had left behind and she'd sprinkled on everything she'd eaten since—it was particularly delicious on eggs and steamed veggies. Or if she was moving out of the morning sickness era of her pregnancy and the other stuff was just coincidence. Either way, she looked forward to the carnival, and the thought of attending it with Viktor put an extra spring in her step. She knew it was dangerous to be so excited to spend the time with him, but she couldn't help herself. Her mind kept drifting to the possibilities. What if he actually started to like her? What if they started a relationship? What if … what if he broke her heart and she had to face him regularly to co-parent this child?

She shook those thoughts away and focused on the idea that they were getting to know each other because they were about to co-parent. No other things should happen. She just needed to keep that firmly in her mind.

She dressed in a rather shapeless sundress because the skirt she'd wanted to wear was a little too tight, but she still managed to feel cute when Viktor knocked on the door.

He looked nervous standing on her porch, his eyes jumped up and down her body, assessing. When he met her eyes his shoulders relaxed, his jaw unclenched, and his lips lifted slightly. "You look like you are feeling better."

"I'm not sure how I should take that," she laughed. "Did I look pretty shitty yesterday?"

His eyes widened in horror. "No! It's just that you were obviously tired and feeling ill. Today you have more color in your cheeks and your eyes are brighter."

She smiled at the compliment and felt her body warm; he was a charming vampire when he wanted to be.

"You know you didn't have to drive here; it would have made more sense for me to meet you at the beach." It was the same sentiment she'd expressed last night when, as promised, he'd called to check on her.

He just shrugged and offered his arm. "I wanted to pick you up. What if you're tired after, I wouldn't want you to drive home sleepy."

That was such a real and honest sentiment showing his care that she felt her heart speed up again despite her determination to keep her mind firmly in the friends category. She had to try really hard to keep herself from feeling like this was a date, especially when he opened and closed the van door for her like a gentleman.

As they drove, Viktor grilled her on what she'd eaten that day and how much she'd slept. That erased the date feelings and turned it into a doctor's appointment. She tried not to be annoyed by the questions and kept reminding herself that he had a reason to care and wasn't just trying to be controlling. She answered, even when she wanted to tell him to shove it, and asked him questions about his day to distract him. He talked excitedly about the surfing he'd done and the group of kids he'd taught a few tricks to when he'd been out there. She realized that he really enjoyed sharing his knowledge of surfing and that was where he found his joy, the same way she found it in painting.

She liked knowing that about him, it felt personal and real. It was beyond the beach bum persona he gave off and far from the spoiled rich senator's kid he could have been. After spending so much time with his sister, she had to wonder if his appearance was created as a way of rebelling against his father and the ideal senator's son. Certainly the senator would have preferred to see his son with a job where he put on a suit every day and carried a briefcase, instead of board shorts and a Hawaiian print shirt.

Chastity had a feeling that the sort of existence his father would have preferred for him would have been a slow death for the happy vampire sitting next to her. She had a lot of respect for him pursuing his dreams like he was, it couldn't have been an easy choice.

When they parked by the beach and the bright lights of the carnival filled the night sky, Chastity's glee had her bouncing in her seat. She loved this tradition. She had dreamed of someday bringing her own family here to mimic what she'd done with her parents so many times as a child. Experiencing the music, rides, games, and greasy food together. She touched her stomach and smiled as she realized she was sort of doing that now with Viktor, and she wondered if they'd ever attend as a family after the child was born. Likely not. She was sure they'd have even less reason to do things together once the baby came, both building a life that included the child but not each other.

It dampened her mood a bit but she had to remind herself that she was not supposed to want to have a relationship with him beyond co-parent. It was more difficult to convince herself of that when he was standing next to her.

"Hey, are you going to be sick?" Viktor asked, coming around the van just then.

"Just a little wave of something, it'll pass," she said with a grimace.

"Are you sure? We don't have to walk through if you're not up to it. I can take you home or to my place, it's close if you need to rest."

"No way, I never miss a carnival," she assured him and started walking toward the beach. What she really needed was a little space from him and a dose of reality.

He hurried to her side, not giving her the space and she didn't ask for it. "Maybe some food will help," he suggested.

"Carnival food is my favorite," she agreed.

They got hot dogs and lemonade and ate as they wandered by booths and lots of happy people.

She stopped to watch the rides as they swirled and turned, the sound of joy and terror filling the night. She smiled up at Viktor who looked particularly dashing in the colored lights.

He was looking down at her and she had the feeling he was going to lean forward, close the minimal distance between them and kiss her. His gaze moved to her mouth and she parted her lips, ready for it. But it wasn't his lips she felt, but his warm finger as it swiped mustard off of her lower lip.

Disappointment she had no right to feel filled her until he stuck that finger into his own mouth and somehow it felt more intimate than a kiss would have in that moment.

"Are you in line?" A group of teens asked breaking the moment.

Viktor answered for them and pulled her out of the way then focused on the ride as if nothing had just happened.

"You don't have to avoid the rides for me," she said, thinking he was watching the ride intently because he wanted on.

"I'm not really a rides person," he admitted.

"You aren't? But you ride waves every day."

"Yes, and nature makes a soft landing in the water. If one of those death contraptions made of metal breaks and I fall, I'll be shattered."

"Wow, I guess I should have read your file. Afraid of carnival rides would have been a deal breaker on choosing your specimen," she teased. "I was going for adventurous."

He rolled his eyes. "And you like to risk your life at the carnival?"

She nodded. "I usually do. I don't get motion sickness easily so I can enjoy the thrill of being tossed around."

"Do you?" he asked, his voice a bit husky and she wondered if he was imagining a very different scenario where she would be tossed a bit.

She certainly was now. Her body heated up and she gulped her lemonade, avoiding eye contact. She cleared her throat. "My father is the same way. We used to do all of the rides together while my mom held our treats for us. She wasn't into the thrill either."

"Smart woman."

"She was," Chastity said, unable to keep the sadness out of her voice. "So, if not the rides, what is it you enjoy about the carnival?"

"The games," he said with pride. "I am an excellent carnival game player."

Chastity laughed. "No one is," she argued. "They're all rigged."

He huffed and put an arm around her shoulders. "I'll prove it," he said and led her toward the stretch of games luring in players with promises of giant stuffed dogs and blow-up aliens.

He ignored the barks of the attendants as he strolled by, seeming to assess each game until he stopped at one where he had to throw a ball through a hole. Seemingly easy, of course, but Chastity knew it would be far from it. These games were all rigged so people lost their money and prizes were rarely given out.

"Three throws for two bucks," the attendant said with a sly

grin at Viktor. "Just get the ball through that there hole and your lady gets to pick a prize." He waved his hand at the array of small to large stuffed prizes.

"My lady deserves a prize, even if she does doubt my skill. Give me three balls," Viktor said, winking at her as he handed the man cash.

The man smiled and wished Viktor good luck as he handed him the balls then stepped out of the way. The man was likely just as doubtful as Chastity that there was going to be any prize handing going on.

The first ball Viktor threw bounced right out of the hole and the attendant made an exaggerated 'aww' and gave him a sympathetic look. "So close, my man."

Chastity rolled her eyes; she'd bet he was already gearing up to try and sell Viktor on more balls to toss.

But the second ball whooshed in without a sound and Chastity couldn't help hopping and clapping as Viktor set the last ball down victorious.

"I see we have a professional, which prize does the lovely lady want?" The attendant said with a practiced smile.

"She'll take that one," Viktor said, pointing to a stuffed vampire doll with fangs and a cape, very *Dracula*.

The attendant passed it over and she grinned up at Viktor, "What if I'd wanted the pink puppy dog?"

"It isn't really for you," he said, lightly touching her stomach.

Chastity's heart flipped, the baby's first present.

"Well then, I suppose it's fitting."

Viktor smiled at her and she couldn't hold back a yawn, which prompted a quick end to their night. Viktor insisted he was tired as well and they'd both had enough excitement. Part of her wanted to argue that he didn't need to baby her, but she *was* tired so she went along with it.

When they got to her place, Viktor walked her to the door and waited while she unlocked it. This felt like a date and suddenly she was riddled with nerves. This is usually where the guy invited himself in or hurried away with a halfhearted assurance to call her. Her fingers shook and she dropped the keys.

Viktor grabbed them quicker than she could react and reached to unlock the door for her and pushed it open. "Are you alright?" he asked, concern making his voice tight and his eyes swept her up and down.

"Yeah, just tired."

"Want me to come in and make you some tea?"

Was that his way of extending their night? Did she want to invite him in? *Invite me in for a nightcap?* Which was code for, *wanna fuck?*

Except as much as it felt like a date, it wasn't, and she knew Viktor's question was exactly what he said. He'd make her tea, hand her a blanket maybe, and then walk out the door.

Why was that so disappointing? Did she really want him to want her, or was she mourning the loss of dating and casual hookups that were nowhere in her future? At least if he said he'd call her, she knew he would.

"It's okay, I think I'll just lay down and sleep till morning."

He nodded but she thought she caught a hint of disappointment there. Had she misread the situation? Was he actually trying to extend this sort of date into her home and bedroom? "But I would love a little tea first, easy enough to make two cups," she said quickly.

Viktor's eyes brightened and he followed her inside.

She went straight to the kitchen and started making tea while he settled into a chair at the table.

"Peppermint okay?"

"Sounds great."

"Why don't we drink it outside, it's such a nice night," she suggested knowing that the kitchen wouldn't get them close enough.

She poured hot water into two cups. One had a heart on it and said *I love dipping my paintbrush in my coffee*, and the other had an image of a cartoon dog. She offered Viktor the one with the dog.

Once settled out on the porch with the sounds of the quiet night surrounding them, they didn't speak for a few minutes. They were on the porch swing and sitting close enough that she could feel the heat coming off his body. The swing wasn't that small. In fact he could scoot over, and they'd be sitting at a distance respectable for friends.

But he'd chosen to sit close, and she hid her smile behind the cup.

His leg twitched and suddenly their knees were touching.

"Do you spend a lot of time in the garden?" he asked as if he could distract her from the obviously intentional move.

She let him have it, she liked his moves. "I don't. I pick stuff that grows well without too much intervention."

"Smart lady."

"I think so," she agreed.

When he turned to her she was smiling up at him. Their eyes met and she felt the spark. That undeniable and unexplainable thrill that encouraged her to tip her chin just a bit more, to lick her lips and leave them slightly parted, inviting. She took a breath, using it to push her chest out slightly. These were her usual moves. They had never failed in getting her at least a hot make out session if not more.

His gaze dipped to her mouth and then lower and back up to her eyes. She knew she had him and she put a daring hand on his thigh.

He took the invitation and leaned down, then they were kissing. His lips were warm and firm, and he used them expertly to apply just the right amount of pressure. She was impatient so she dipped her tongue out to run across his bottom lip where he tasted like peppermint.

He pulled away as her tongue tried to invade his mouth. "Chastity, wait," he said, his words slightly distorted and his face flushed.

Embarrassment flooded her, oh god, she'd just thrown herself at him, what was she thinking? "Oh, sorry, I just—"

"No," he stopped her, "don't start doing that. I kissed you; I wanted to, *very much*. It's just that, well, I don't know if this is a great idea."

"Because your fangs are out?" she had thought that was a good sign, kind of like a boner, it showed he was aroused by her, right? But maybe she was wrong. Maybe he was hungry and she was inadvertently tempting him to bite her.

A part of her was very into that idea.

"No, that happens." He shrugged and his cheeks tinged pink.

"Is it because I'm pregnant?" she was ready to be offended if that was his problem, it was his baby after all.

"No! Goddess no, that doesn't make you any less attractive, it's just that I don't want to mess up. We are going to be in each other's lives for the long haul."

Chastity hated that he was right. If they slept together tonight, it could end badly and they wouldn't be able to just cut each other out of their lives. If they stopped now, it would end with her and her showerhead, a much safer option in the long run.

Viktor gave her an apologetic smile and stood offering his hand. She let him help her up. "Thanks for joining me tonight, and for the tea, it was really nice," he said.

"No problem, I had a great time too." She took his half empty cup and stepped away before she could throw herself at him again. "I'll see you at your sister's for dinner tomorrow night."

"Right. I can pick you up, it's on my way."

"That would be good, if you don't mind."

"Not at all. Make sure you take your supplements before bed," he said then turned and walked away.

She shook her head and walked inside, disappointed and

wanting. But she knew it was for the best. He wasn't interested in dating her so it would have been a one-night stand. She looked down at the vampire doll that she'd left lying on the kitchen table. He hadn't even won a prize for her; it was for the baby. She needed to be careful she didn't read into his behavior. This wasn't a relationship; this was a co-parenting situation. And although he was a normal male who responded to sexual advances, it didn't mean he wanted to change that situation.

Viktor sat in his van for a minute just staring at her house. His hands gripped the wheel and he clenched his teeth. His instincts were telling him to go in there and lay claim to the little beauty, to make her his. But was it just because she was carrying his baby? She was undeniably attractive and the kiss had been amazing, but the need he was feeling went beyond just wanting to be with her once or twice and he wasn't used to that. He wanted to make sure she was his in every way and keep everyone else at bay. He wanted to cover her in his scent and his bites. He wanted to announce to the world that she was off limits, that she belonged to him.

He grunted and started the van. It had to be just because of the baby she was carrying; he didn't get possessive about women. He liked to keep things casual and fun, no attachments, no promises, and when they were done, they were done, no big deal. This kept everyone from getting hurt.

Including him.

With Chastity it was even more complicated than usual. She was carrying his child and he'd never intended to try and have a relationship with the woman who bore his child, that was the whole point of having his sperm stored at the clinic. He wanted a child through a business-like arrangement, no feelings need apply.

"Fucking Moon Goddess," he cursed as he drove home.

CHAPTER SIXTEEN

"What do you mean you kissed him?" Martha demanded with a squeal of excitement. They were on video chat because Chastity needed help picking out something to wear for the dinner party. As soon as Martha had seen Chastity's face she'd demanded to know what had happened. Apparently, her face looked far too happy about a night that should be nerve wracking at best.

"Just that. We were sitting on the porch swing drinking tea and it just happened."

"Who started it?"

"I don't know, I think we both sort of did."

"And you ended it?"

"Him," she admitted with a sigh. "Which was a good thing. We shouldn't complicate things with sex, there's a child to consider."

"There's also an attraction that you two are going to have to deal with, that's not just going to go away, Chastity."

"You're right, but it's also not what tonight is about, so what do I wear?" Nothing had felt right that she'd tried on so far. It was all too tight or too casual. So much had paint splatters because when she felt inspired she rarely took the time to change her clothes before painting.

"Take me to your closet, let's see what you have," Martha instructed, and Chastity was thankful that her friend was letting the kiss go, at least for the moment.

Dressed only in black lace panties and matching bra, Chastity hurried into her closet and flipped the light on. She toured Martha around and groaned about the need to go shopping. Chastity dressed casual pretty much every day, but tonight definitely needed something special.

"What's that blue one down there, looks like it has a black pattern," Martha asked.

"Let me pull it out." Chastity hurried to set Martha down on a shelf with a view of the closet and turned to grab the blue dress. How she'd spotted the thing buried on a bottom rung, Chastity had no idea, but that's why she'd called for help. Martha had an eye for fashion that Chastity wasn't born with, and it helped that she literally had better eyesight than Chastity. Chastity bent in half and pushed aside clothes she hadn't looked at in ages.

A groaned, *"Fuck,"* had Chastity jumping and spinning.

When she saw that somehow the video call was now with Viktor she screamed and threw herself at the phone, knocking it onto the floor.

Unfortunately, it landed facing up from her feet giving him a clear view of her lace-covered crotch.

All she saw before stomping on the damn thing was Viktor's slack jawed face, a hint of fang, and eyes wide and black.

She wanted to die.

She ran out of the closet and threw herself on her bed, burrowing under the covers. She would just stay there until she died, she decided. How long did it take to die from embarrassment? She put the pillow over her head and waited for the mortification to kill her.

Eventually she had to admit she wasn't going to be saved by a quick death, so she got up and wrapped herself chin to toe in a blanket then went for the phone.

Thank Goddess the screen was black.

She looked across the closet at the blue dress now laying on the floor. It was short and flirty; it had thin straps and a modest neckline. It would be perfect for a date and appropriate for a family dinner. But she hung it back up, she wanted to be covered fully now. She pulled out a pair of flowy black slacks and a simple white t-shirt. She'd dress it up with heels and jewelry.

And she'd wear a sweater, she didn't want to show *any* skin.

"Dude, are you okay?"

Viktor looked over the counter at his longtime friend, Jason, and blinked. Closing his lips and willing his fangs to retract, he took a few breaths and swallowed the lump in his throat. He was thankful for the counter hiding the other part of him that had reacted in the extreme to the sight of Chastity's fucking perfect ass wiggling in black lace and then when she'd turned! Oh gods he'd gotten an eyeful of her breasts, swollen and busting out of the bra and then when she'd dropped the phone all he could focus on was that heart shaped birthmark and he was done for.

"No," Viktor croaked.

"Do you have some chick sending you nudes or something? I haven't seen a reaction that fast since freshman year of college."

Viktor scowled at Jason, but his friend only laughed.

"No judgment. I wish I could get that excited about anyone these days. So, you gonna tell me who it is? Some tourist, or a local?"

Viktor hadn't told Jason about his situation, and he didn't want to now, either. He didn't want to explain his relationship with Chastity or minimize it. Didn't want to … what? Admit it wasn't a relationship? Or didn't want to admit he wanted a relationship?

"No one you know," Viktor snapped and went back to pulling inventory out of a box.

"Oh, possessive," Jason laughed. "Now I'm very intrigued. Maybe I'll accept your father's invitation to dinner tonight, are you bringing this *no one?*"

Viktor's eyes snapped up and he narrowed them at his friend. "Why the hell would my father invite you to dinner tonight?" His father had never liked Jason. He had always said Jason was a waste of good vampire blood, kind of like Viktor.

"Because he wanted me to bring Sara."

Viktor rolled his eyes. Of course. His father had been trying to get Viktor interested in Jason's sister for years. It was Johnson's dream to unite the two families in marriage. Jason and Sara's father was an important vampire and political ally in the city.

Viktor had never had any interest in being a pawn in his father's political games, and now more than ever had no interest in dating Sara.

"Don't come," Viktor snapped.

"Too late, already texted Sara, she's excited, she loves your sister."

Viktor hissed at his friend, who laughed, then sobered at the look of murder Viktor wasn't hiding.

"Hey, relax man. I'm always on your side, you know that. Let me be a buffer between you and your father. Whatever, or whoever, you're hiding, you don't want your father focused on it, do you?"

Viktor relaxed, Jason was right, the more people to distract from Chastity the better. He gave Jason a brief explanation of the situation.

"Well shit, congratulations man. This is exciting news."

"Is it?"

"And if she's hot, well that's even better."

"It's a complication," Viktor said.

"Is it?" Jason asked, turning Viktor's words back on him and then walked out. "See you tonight."

Viktor stared after his friend. The excited reaction wasn't what he had expected, and it eased something in his chest. He'd been holding back from telling anyone because he'd been worried about how people would perceive the situation. Having his best friend's acceptance felt like the support he needed to make his situation public.

His thoughts returned to what he'd seen on the screen to start that whole ordeal and his fangs ached once again and his shorts tightened.

"Fuck," he hissed and closed the shop in a hurry. He would need a cold shower before he picked Chastity up.

He dressed in black slacks and a black button up with little gray palm trees all over it. Then he stopped and purchased flowers for his sister and some for Chastity. On a whim he also grabbed a couple steaks.

He enjoyed the thought of nourishing his child through her. And since watching her devour the steak he'd cooked for her he hasn't been able to get the image out of his mind. She'd been so focused on eating she thankfully hadn't noticed how enraptured he'd been in the scene. He'd had to grip the chair to keep from leaping forward to lick the juices from her plump lips and each time she swallowed he swore he could feel the movement of her throat as if it were rippling over his cock. He could have watched that scene forever and wanted a repeat so badly he'd had to force himself not to invite himself over to cook in her kitchen again. He was sure he'd be unable to resist her a second time. Watching her eat at the carnival had been almost as bad, but being in public helped him to control the lustful thoughts. Tonight would be far too distracting with his father around for her eating to affect him.

But here he was buying steaks in the hopes of torturing himself in the near future with watching her eat it. Maybe he was a masochist.

CHAPTER SEVENTEEN

Chastity had debated canceling the entire time she'd gotten ready, but when she saw Viktor standing on her porch with reddened cheeks and gifts in hand, she was glad she hadn't.

"You didn't have to bring me anything," she whispered as she took the flowers.

"Meat, I want to make sure you and the baby are getting enough fresh meat to keep healthy. I'd be happy to cook it for you again," he added as he walked past her to the kitchen.

Chastity followed and grabbed a vase for the flowers; appreciating that she had something to do while she tried to calm her racing heart. It was going to be a long night if she didn't just acknowledge what had happened earlier.

"I was on video call with Martha. She was helping me pick out an outfit for tonight. I don't know how I ended up calling you. I'm really sorry," she said as she fiddled with the flowers in the vase and added water, not daring to look in his direction as he put the steaks in the refrigerator.

Viktor cleared his throat. "Quite alright," he said, his voice husky.

Chastity looked up from the flowers and met his gaze. His

eyes were dark, and his lids half closed. She felt his gaze like a caress and her body responded with pleasurable warmth.

"I wasn't trying to show you my ass or anything on purpose," she mumbled.

He groaned and turned around. "We should go," he said, his words slurred, and she wondered if his fangs had popped out, but if they had that would mean ...

Was he excited by the memory of her body? She looked down at the flowers. Was this a date?

She grabbed her purse with a new smile on her face and met him at the door. When they got to his van he opened the passenger door for her. This was definitely feeling like a date, and she couldn't convince herself that it was a bad idea.

They didn't talk as they drove, Viktor seemed distracted, and Chastity concentrated on the music. They were stopped by security at the end of Persia's driveway, something she hadn't ever encountered on her many visits here. They were asked to show their identification to a large man with dark sunglasses on despite the fact that the sun was down.

"Does your father always bring security to your sister's house?"

Viktor grunted. "He brings security everywhere. I think it makes him feel important more than keeps him safe."

Chastity nodded and noted the men stationed around the property, all wearing black suits and sunglasses like the guy at the gate.

"Doesn't everyone love him? He's done a lot for vampire and werewolf rights. I think even the witches are pro-Paulie."

"Depends on who you ask. Progressives love him, conservatives don't. Like any public figure there's no consensus. I suppose if there was then he'd be out of a job."

Chastity understood that Viktor didn't get along well with his father, but she also knew it wasn't about his political views. Which meant it was likely just the usual parent/child relationship stuff. Overbearing parents trying to live their life through their kids, or wanting what they thought was the best for their children, despite what their children might want.

"I'm excited to meet Persia's husband, he's never been here when I'm painting."

"He's a nice guy, not as stuffy as most city vampires. I'm sure you'll meet a lot of people tonight who have sticks up their asses, my father never travels alone. I am sorry it won't be just family; it's not like you really need to be involved in all this political maneuvering."

Chastity was actually relieved to hear that, maybe it would take some of the pressure off of her. They could do intimate family gatherings later on if necessary. Would it be necessary? Not really if they were just doing a split family situation. She glanced at Viktor, he was very handsome tonight, if they dated she'd certainly get to know his father on a more personal level.

This was not going to be personal at all judging by the number of cars parked around the driveway. "Wow," she said as they parked.

"Yeah," he grumbled.

She didn't wait for him to get her door once he turned off the van because she didn't want to assume anything, but he offered his arm as they approached the house and she latched on, feeling nervous to be introduced to so many new people.

"Do they all know about me, about us, and this?" she waved at her belly.

"I doubt it. My father will be trying to control the information and how and when it goes public," Viktor scoffed. "So don't expect anyone to congratulate you or ask about the baby."

She wasn't sure if she was glad about that or not. So was she supposed to be Viktor's date? Or just a random person invited to this party?

"Chastity!" Persia exclaimed as soon as they entered the house. Persia threw her arms around Chastity, forcing her to let go of Viktor. "Thank goddess you're here, my father keeps trying to talk to me about having another baby. I need a distraction." Persia was dressed in a black cocktail dress that was far more formal than what Chastity was wearing and she regretted not going with the dress.

Chastity laughed nervously and touched her belly. "Happy to help, I think."

"You'll regret that," Viktor mumbled, and Persia stuck her tongue out at him then grabbed Chastity's arm and led her into the other room where music and conversation threatened to overwhelm her. She did a quick scan of the room, it seemed everyone in it was dressed much finer than her, all in expensive-looking suits and dresses. She felt out of place in so many ways, and she wanted to go back to clinging to Viktor's arm.

"Look who's arrived, the lady of the hour," Persia announced.

The conversations silenced briefly and all eyes turned to her. She felt like she was going to pass out as gazes assessed her. Thankfully most went right back to what they were already doing and ignored her.

It was easy to spot Johnson Paulie, senator and grandfather to her unborn child, among the crowd. He was tall and broad and oozed importance in a dark red suit with a black tie. His gaze stayed on her and promised many questions that she likely didn't have the right answers to. No one else in the room was familiar to her. They all seemed to be vampires though and she felt like a virgin going to sacrifice.

Viktor put a hand to her lower back and she looked up at him, pleading.

He just gave her a tight smile and pushed her towards his father. "Let's get this over with," he whispered.

Viktor smiled and nodded to everyone who greeted him as they crossed the room, it seemed he knew everyone here. When they got to the senator, Chastity was sweating and thought she might pass out. "Father, this is Chastity Martin, she's pregnant with my child."

"Yes, how exciting this is. A little half-human will look wonderful on my next campaign, when are you due?"

Chastity had to clear her throat before she could speak. "April," she said with a tight smile, trying to ignore his comment about his campaign.

"Splendid, tell me, what do you do? Some kind of artist I hear," he asked with what seemed like genuine interest.

Chastity relaxed into the familiar topic as she talked of her art and he even asked to see the mural she was currently working on for Persia. She was in her element with this conversation and she felt nothing but friendly curiosity from the man. "I'd love to show it to you." And she'd love to get a little fresh air and quiet, the room was very loud with so many conversations going on.

Johnson offered her his arm and she took it with a smile, this was so much easier than anything she'd imagined meeting Viktor's father was going to be. She wasn't even sweating anymore.

Viktor moved to follow them as they headed outside but his father gave him a harsh look. "You need to go chat with Sara. Be a good second host for your sister, you know her husband isn't worthy of the task," Johnson said in a tone that left no room for argument.

Johnson led her away, clearly not considering that Viktor would refuse his order, or that she might not want to be alone with him. Chastity looked back and gave Viktor a little smile, she wasn't worried about showing Johnson the mural and if it would keep an argument from happening then Viktor should go find whoever it was that his father thought he needed to.

Viktor gave her a small nod and moved across the room to the obvious delight of a vampire with long black hair and a dress that was cut low and high, revealing so much skin she likely could have been comfortable on a beach. She was lovely and embraced

Viktor immediately, kissing his cheek and whispering in his ear familiarly.

Chastity felt something in her stomach twist at the sight, but she ignored it as she went with a smile plastered on her face, because she knew she had no real claim over Viktor. The way he'd let the woman rub against him made that very clear. Had his father known what he was sending his son to? Obviously the man knew that she and Viktor weren't a couple, so why not send him in the direction of a young and available woman? Wasn't it a parent's prerogative to see their offspring married and happy?

Chastity suddenly felt ill and gulped in the fresh air when they got outside.

"Are you alright?" Johnson asked.

"Yeah, just pregnancy, you know," she said with a little laugh then motioned to the mural. She didn't want to have a conversation with Johnson about her feelings at the moment. She launched into an explanation of what she planned for the space but he no longer seemed at all interested in her art, just eyed her curiously as she talked. Finally she stopped and faced him fully, not willing to keep up what was apparently a charade.

"It's quite favorable to have been accidentally impregnated by such an important man as my son," he said when she stopped talking.

Chastity froze.

"Don't get me wrong, I am glad you are a human, but still, you're a nobody."

"I—I," she stuttered, trying to come up with some kind of statement to refute what he was saying. It was such a vast turn from what he'd been saying inside. Of course, out here, there was no one to overhear.

"God knows why my son decided to keep his sperm in that place to begin with. He should have waited until a proper marriage or at least a suitable couple approached him with an offer, but what is done is done. So, I am going to support you. I am going to embrace the child, and I am going to make sure you get what you wanted out of this ordeal, Chastity Martin. But you are going to sign this first." He pulled a document and pen out of his pocket.

"I don't think Viktor—"

He cut her off with a hiss. "Viktor relies on me for these things. He wants to keep his little life surfing, banging beach babes, and being the epitome of disappointment to his father. He is going to do that, and I am going to take the responsibility of the child, that's the deal," he said dismissively and shoved the papers at her.

Chastity was beyond confused. This couldn't be what Viktor wanted. Could it?

A lump formed in her throat and her stomach cramped. She was impressed that she managed to speak with little shake to her voice. "I will have to look these over when I have time." Her mind was spinning and her stomach was ready to unload everything in it. She was half tempted to do just that right on the man's expensive suit or shoes.

Johnson sighed heavily. "If you must. But be aware that if you want any help with that thing, you are going to have to get it from me and not that idiot son of mine who is currently trying to get that slutty vampire into his sister's guest bed." He chuckled and nodded toward the house. "Sara and he have always had a thing, I don't understand why they don't make it official, but," he shrugged, "kids are just so damn stubborn sometimes. Perhaps soon they'll agree and do what we all know they will do eventually, she has a fertile body I'm told, very important in a vampire wife."

Chastity felt her stomach twist again and she was sure she was going to puke. Had she eaten enough today to puke up anything other than acid and water? She had been nervous about tonight, plus the whole phone incident, and she always had a hard time eating when she was nervous.

"I think I need some water," she whispered, hating how frail her voice sounded. She clasped her hands to stop them from shaking, she didn't want to show weakness in front of this predator.

Johnson gave her a slick smile and put an arm around her back, leading her inside and stuffing the papers in her purse as they went.

"Of course, water for the pregnant human, how quaint."

As soon as they were back in the room with everyone else, Johnson abandoned Chastity, his mission, apparently, over. She looked around desperately but didn't see Viktor anywhere. She also didn't see the gorgeous vampire, Sara, he'd been talking with. Tears stung her eyes and she berated herself for being so stupid. Of course Viktor didn't like her, didn't want her. He probably was just being extra nice tonight so she'd sign the damn papers his father had been planning to shove at her.

She needed to get out of there. She looked around desperate for any face she recognized but there was no one. She didn't even see Persia anywhere.

Chastity pulled her phone out as she headed for the front door. She would call a ride and maybe never talk to Viktor again unless it was through a lawyer.

Stumbling out the front door with tears starting to leak from her eyes, bile rose in her throat and her blood rushed through her veins. She ran to the side of the porch and unloaded the little that had been in her stomach. As she'd suspected, it was mostly just stomach acid and it burned her throat as it came up.

"Hey, you must be Viktor's human," a voice said when she stood and used the hem of her sweater to wipe her face. She spun around, full of mortification but the sudden movement was too much for her and she felt too light, her eyes darkened and she started to swoon.

"Fuck," she whispered as she listed to the side.

"Shit, are you okay?" the man asked, putting an arm around her.

"No, I need to go home."

"Okay, no big deal, I'll grab Viktor."

"No!" she yelled, and he stiffened.

She pulled away, wobbling slightly. "I'm calling a ride, he's … busy."

The man, vampire obviously, nodded. "I'll give you a ride, come on."

She was too desperate to get away to consider the possibilities of being murdered by a stranger, so she let the man guide her to a small sportscar and settled into the seat. She sighed with relief when he closed the door, shutting out the noise from the house.

He got in the driver's seat and started up the car. She didn't know much about cars, but she could tell whatever this was, it was expensive, and she really hoped she didn't puke in it. She closed her eyes and laid her head back.

"I'm Jason," he said after a few minutes.

"Chastity," she said.

"I figured," he laughed. "Where do you live?"

She gave him her address and brief directions. Her phone started to ring but she ignored it, she knew who it was, and she had no desire to talk to him. It paused and rang again. Jason looked at her curiously, but she just scowled back and he huffed a laugh. A text chimed next and she groaned.

Jason's phone rang then, and his radio announced that *Vik the dick* was calling.

"Please don't answer," she pleaded, and he nodded, hitting ignore.

"You wanna talk about it?"

"No."

"Cool. But you know he's probably going to show up at your house a few minutes after us, right?"

"Don't see why he'd bother," she snapped, but then

remembered the papers in her purse and realized he might, because she hadn't signed them yet. "Can you actually take me to my friend's place instead," she asked. She couldn't face Viktor tonight.

"Anything you need, Chastity."

Twenty minutes later, Chastity was running into Martha's waiting arms. Martha's husband and two of her brothers were standing on the porch, arms crossed and glaring.

Jason waved from the car, knowing better than to walk uninvited into a werewolf den.

"Who's that jackass?" Martha's brother, Luke, snarled.

"Want me to bite him?" Martha's other brother, Tony, snapped.

"Thanks boys, but that's not the one who made Chastity cry," Martha said.

Chastity pulled away from Martha as Jason drove away. "I just needed to not be at home where he could find me tonight," Chastity said.

"Understood, give me your phone."

Chastity was happy to hand it over.

Martha turned the power off and stuffed it in her pocket. "Let's get you something to eat."

Chastity let herself be led into the house and be taken care of. Maybe it was the cowardly way to react, but she didn't care. She'd be tough tomorrow or maybe the next day, but tonight, she needed someone else to be strong for her and she didn't know anyone stronger than Martha and Elaine.

Elaine came roaring through the house and embraced her. "What sort of horrible man would make a pregnant woman cry?" she snarled.

"Powerful men and their small dick energy," Martha offered making Chastity laugh.

That one laugh was all it took to reassure Chastity that she *would* be okay. This night had sucked, it had changed everything and she was going to be sad tonight about it. But she'd be okay because her best friend could still make her laugh.

Viktor didn't care if he was being crazy, he found an open window in Chastity's studio and climbed in so he could get to her. Unfortunately, a quick walkthrough of the house revealed that she wasn't home despite her car still being in the driveway.

He sat on the front porch to wait. How had he made it here before them? Jason wasn't answering his phone, and neither was Chastity. He imagined horrifying scenarios where Jason charmed her, stopped somewhere secluded and—he couldn't even let his mind finish that without wanting to feel his best friend's last pulse stop under his palms or teeth.

Viktor dropped his head in his hands and tried to breathe through the fear and anger. He had been so stupid. He knew better than to trust his father. Knew he shouldn't have let Chastity be alone with the man, but he didn't want to cause a scene, and she'd seemed confident. So he'd gone to chat with Sara, who had looked at him like he was a bloody steak, and she was fangs out for him.

He wasn't interested, but he couldn't be rude at his sister's party. His childhood social training drilled so deep into him that he had offered to get her a drink and had chatted with her politely. When she'd asked him to take her on a little tour of Persia's night garden he'd done so reluctantly.

Of course, once out in the garden she'd tried to throw herself at him and turning her down had made her laugh and shrug. She'd admitted that his father had bribed her to try and seduce him. She wasn't interested in an arranged marriage with Viktor but she admitted that a roll in the hay was intriguing, so she'd taken the deal.

In the end they'd strolled in a friendly manner around the garden. When Viktor had walked back inside to find his father chatting with his cronies and Chastity nowhere in sight, it hadn't taken long to find out she'd left with Jason. But he had no idea why, and he didn't have time to force answers out of his father, so he'd driven here as fast as possible.

Viktor's phone rang and he answered immediately without even looking at the screen. "Chastity?"

"Nope, but close, I'm just as adorable," Jason said.

"Where the hell are you guys?"

"I am on my way home after dropping her off with some nice werewolves she knows."

"What the fuck happened?" Viktor demanded.

"I was going to ask you the same thing. That girl almost passed out on Persia's porch after puking her guts out. She was white as a vampire and looked scared and pissed, and man, she was cute too. I can see why you're so obsessed."

"Jason," Viktor snapped. "What made her leave? If she was just feeling ill, she wouldn't be ignoring my calls."

"No, I had a feeling it was something you did."

"More like my father," he hissed. "Okay, I know who she's with, I bet I can look up an address."

"Yeah, surrounded by protective wolves. You aren't getting to her tonight man. Give her a minute to calm down from whatever happened."

Viktor hated to admit Jason was probably right. It killed him to know she was hurting and angry, that he hadn't protected her from the one person he knew was likely to be an asshole.

He pulled out his phone and sent an angry text to his father.

> What the hell did you do to Chastity?

His reply was everything Viktor had come to expect from the man.

I did what you should have done day one. I gave her a realistic contract to sign.

"Fuck!" Viktor shouted into the night. She was never going to trust him if she thought he'd sent his father on that mission. He didn't even need to know the details of the contract to know it was going to be unfair to Chastity and the child, likely to him too. The only thing Johnson Paulie cared about was his public image and the power he gained from it.

She had to believe he hadn't been a part of that, right? She wouldn't think he agreed with whatever crazy scheme his father had come up with, would she?

He hated that he wasn't sure.

He leaned back and stared up at the sky as the swing moved gently. The last time he'd sat on this swing he'd been so happy. Now he felt like everything he wanted out of life was once again being pulled away by his father. When his father had inserted himself into Viktor's life to this degree before, Viktor had disappeared for a year and traveled the world, surfing waves. This time he couldn't run; he had to stay and protect what he wanted.

He wanted Chastity and he wanted their baby, a fact that had never been more clear to him than when he'd raced from his sister's house terrified that their budding relationship had been extinguished.

CHAPTER EIGHTEEN

Chastity ignored Viktor's calls for the next month and a half. She texted him once a week to let him know how she was doing; always fine. She'd asked that he respect her decision to stay away for now. He tried to say he had nothing to do with his father's plan and the girl he'd been talking to was nothing to him, but she didn't care to believe him. And it didn't really matter. All that mattered was the baby and what was best for it. She reminded him that they didn't need to even be friends to raise this child, and she'd figure out some kind of legal documents before the birth for them to agree to. Some kind of custodial rights agreement and visitation arrangement. None of that was necessary before the child was born though and she was certainly not signing anything that his father shoved at her.

At least he had the decency to tell her to burn those papers and ignore anything else his father might send her way.

Viktor assured her that he would agree to whatever she wanted, whatever she thought was best for the child. He told her that he would be there for her and the child as much as she'd let him be. She had a feeling those claims would change as soon as she shoved a paper at him that stated a parenting plan of her own choosing, which would in no way include public appearances or political rallies.

She went to two doctor appointments alone but sent him updates and pictures. He had groceries, blood builder vitamins, and blood spice delivered to her house, which she appreciated. He cared about the child, that much was obvious. It had been her mistake to start thinking that he cared about her too.

She still found herself hoping and worrying every time a car door slammed outside, or someone knocked. Would he show up despite her firm instructions not to? And every day he didn't appear at her house she told herself she was glad, but a part of her was disappointed. It only further proved he was only interested in the child and what it meant to his family. He wasn't fighting to be a part of her life.

What else had she expected though? He'd given his sperm to the clinic so that he could have a child with another couple. He never wanted a partner with a child.

As she stood in her studio staring at a black-prepped canvas trying to figure out what she'd been thinking when she started, her phone rang and her heart started beating quickly in anticipation, but it was only Martha.

"Happy second trimester!" Martha squealed.

"Yay," she said with a sigh and rubbed her slightly rounded belly. She was happy to finally be showing, and her nausea had mostly stopped a week ago.

"This means you need to sign up for birthing classes and start decorating the nursery, you also need to invest in batteries because you're going to be horny."

"Wonderful, how are you doing?"

"Big and angry about it," Martha admitted. "This is my last month, so I know I'm not going to feel great, but I was hoping I'd feel better than this."

Chastity had sympathy for her friend but also envied her

being near the end of the pregnancy and almost being able to see and hold the little angel.

"Have you decided if you're going to find out the gender tomorrow?"

Chastity sighed. "I'm still not sure if I want to know."

"Are you going to ask Viktor to go in with you?"

Chastity just grunted. She had been debating that too but figured if she wasn't finding out the gender then there was no reason to include him.

"I don't see why he needs to be there either way," she lied.

"Sure, okay honey. Well if you need me to go with you, just call. I love you."

"Love you too, Martha, get some rest."

"Get some batteries!" Martha laughed and hung up.

Chastity set down her phone and picked up her brush, then dipped it into a silver paint. She let her hand move without much thought, bringing bold strokes over the canvas until it shaped a heavy breast and rounded belly.

A self portrait.

"Viktor, dude you look like shit."

Viktor looked up from the counter where he'd been staring at an inventory list without actually seeing it. All he saw was the date. Today marked Chastity's second trimester and he hadn't seen her in over a month.

Jason waltzed in with a wide smile and Viktor wanted to punch him for no reason other than the fact that he was happy and worry free.

"I don't feel like company," he said.

"I know, you said that every time I texted since I dropped your incubator off, but I have a feeling you don't actually mean it."

Viktor clenched his teeth at Jason's term for Chastity. She

wasn't just an incubator for his child, she was—she was a wonderful person, a beautiful soul, and she was going to be the mother of his child.

"*There's* a bit of fire," Jason said. "Now, what can we do to get you out of this slump? I know lots of easy women. We can have a party. Or we can walk the beach and pick up tourists, offer them free riding lessons," Jason said with a wiggle of his eyebrows.

"Not interested," Viktor snapped. He hadn't had sex since he found out about Chastity and that could definitely be a leading factor in his grumpiness. But he wasn't interested in solving that. No one tempted him, except Chastity. He dreamed about her nearly every night and woke up aching with need for her, no substitute was going to satisfy him.

"No? Well then how about a beer?" Jason held up a six pack Viktor hadn't even noticed was in his hand.

"Sure," Viktor said and walked out to the small table and chairs set out on the porch of the store.

Once settled, both sipping and staring out at the ocean as the sun started to set, Jason spoke, this time his tone was serious.

"Did you ever find out what your father did?"

"He tried to get her to sign a contract allowing him to use the child as part of his upcoming campaigns in exchange for an allowance. And of course, giving me fifty percent custody which he would have actually taken."

"Shit."

"Yeah."

"No wonder she was upset, but why is she so mad at you? You aren't in control of what your father does."

"He convinced her I was off fucking Sara while he was shoving the contract in her face."

"Damn, that's harsh."

"But she believed it," he shook his head, hurt by her willingness to believe what his father had been feeding her.

"She barely knows you, she's pregnant, and probably more

than a little freaked out by everything. Can you really blame her for jumping to the wrong conclusions? Especially coming from your father, he's made a life out of lying convincingly."

Viktor sighed. "No, I can't blame her for believing him in that moment. But even now she refuses to believe anything I tell her. She should have realized by now that my father was lying."

"Maybe she has but still, she never wanted a baby's father, Viktor, so she doesn't see the value in welcoming you into her life."

Viktor couldn't even blame her for that, what had he really offered her?

"You will be able to be a part of the child's life when it comes around, right?"

"Yes, she has agreed to that. We'll make a contract of some kind, of her choosing, I owe her that."

"Okay so what's the problem?"

The problem was that it wasn't enough. He didn't just want to be a part of the child's life, he wanted to be a part of Chastity's life.

Jason looked at him expectantly and raised an eyebrow. "Because she makes your fangs hard, huh, drops them like a frisky teen?"

Viktor just grunted and took a swig of his beer.

"Damn. I suppose if I found a girl that could do that for me at this point in my life I'd be chasing her too. You could always just fuck her and get it out of your system."

Viktor hissed at Jason who put up his hands in defense.

"Hey, it's usually enough to bed a girl once, why not with her?"

"Because I don't want things to be awkward. We are going to be parenting a child together. That matters more than my dick."

"Wow, never thought I'd hear you say anything mattered more than where you could stick your dick."

"Neither did I," Viktor admitted and finished his beer, then grabbed another one. Maybe he could drink away the pain and confusion.

"So what are you going to do?" Jason asked after they'd both finished their second beers.

"Whatever she'll let me."

CHAPTER NINETEEN

Chastity sat in the waiting room staring at her phone. She should text him, but it was a little late for that, wasn't it? He'd never get here in time anyway.

She shoved it back in her bag and picked up a magazine and flipped through it without seeing any of the pictures. Until one caught her attention. There was Johnson Paulie standing in front of the Stonecroft Clinic with a huge smile on his face and the witch sisters who owned the place. The title of the article declared: *An Artificial Insemination Miracle Brings Humans And Vampires Closer Than Ever.*

Chastity quickly scoured the article for any mention of herself or Viktor. It was mostly vague, thank goddess. It spoke of the clinic favorably, highlighting how it was specializing in both human and vampire fertilization. Not damning by itself but then at the end she felt her stomach drop. It said that Johnson would soon be announcing his son's good news, thanks to the clinic.

"Shit," Chastity hissed and pulled out her phone to text Viktor. Had he seen this, did he know what his father had been up to? She froze, staring down at Viktor's name. He probably knew. Of course he knew. Why wouldn't he? She was pissed.

Why hadn't he warned her? How could he have kept something like this from her and how long before her pregnancy was splashed all over the news without her agreement?

"Ms. Martin," the nurse called.

Chastity snatched up the magazine and stuffed it, and her phone, into her bag before she hurried toward the nurse holding the door open with a big smile.

"Just you today?" she asked. She always asked the same thing.

"Just me and the baby," Chastity corrected with a nervous laugh and the woman didn't try hard enough to hide her look of sympathy.

Chastity wanted to defend herself, she didn't need or want a partner in this. Certainly didn't want to sacrifice her child to a political campaign just to have someone hold her hand.

She pushed thoughts of the article from her mind as the doctor did his exam and took ultrasound images of the growing child. She decided she didn't want to know right then what it was, but had him write it down and put it in an envelope for her. She would be able to know at any moment, and that felt like enough for now.

"Everything is growing right on schedule, you're doing great," he assured her before walking out of the room.

Tears stung her eyes and she felt like an idiot for crying at those words, but she'd needed them. She *was* doing a good job.

She hurried to get out of there and headed straight for Mooncalled Coffee. She needed to share the article with Martha before it completely spiraled her into panic.

When she arrived at the coffee shop Martha motioned for her to sit outside and waddled out to join her a few minutes later. Glen followed with a cup of herbal tea for each of them. He gave his wife a sympathetic kiss as she groaned about how uncomfortable she was.

"More uncomfortable than you should be?" Chastity asked with concern.

"No, but I wouldn't be surprised if this little pup came early, I feel like a bowling ball is wedged between my legs," Martha groaned and rubbed at her belly.

"Well, I come with distractions, take a look at this," Chastity said, slapping the magazine between them. It was open to the article and Martha's eyes widened as she grabbed it. Her mouth hung open as she read.

"I found that in the waiting room," Chastity said when Martha looked up from the magazine.

"Oh my goddess," she growled.

"Yeah."

"Do you think he knows?"

"I don't see how he couldn't."

Martha looked ready to kick some ass despite being about to give birth and Chastity appreciated the support.

"Next time he comes in, I'll spit in his coffee."

Chastity laughed. "Well, it's not worth losing your business license over, but maybe you can at least have Glen growl in his direction."

"Of course, that goes without saying. That vampire will never feel comfortable here again."

Chastity smiled at her friend and sipped her tea. This was the type of support a girl needed.

"Are you going to call him?"

"I don't know. A part of me wants to confront him, and part of me wants to wait and see how long before he tells me himself."

"I think you should demand answers while you're mad, because I know you, Chastity. If you wait long enough to let things settle you'll come up with all kinds of excuses for him and he'll get away with being an asshole."

Chastity couldn't even argue with that, she knew Martha was right.

"He deserves your anger, Chastity."

"But anger hurts me just as much as him, and I don't want the baby to develop in an angry womb."

"Oh, speaking of baby, did you find out? Pink or blue?"

"I had him write it down, I didn't think I was in the right frame of mind to appreciate the answer right then."

Martha nodded as if that made perfect sense. "Did you buy batteries?" Martha asked, changing the subject so quick Chastity nearly spit out her tea.

"I have everything I need," she confessed. Mostly she preferred to masturbate in the shower with the massaging showerhead but she had purchased something Martha had recommended, just in case.

"I'm sure I can find you a date, Glen's cousin has a thing for pregnant women and he's not looking for a relationship."

"No thanks." The thought of casual sex held no appeal and she wondered if she'd ever be back to a place where casual hookups were on the table. It didn't seem like something a parent would do, then again, maybe it was exactly what a single parent does because dating would be even harder than usual. She assumed that once she felt good in her body again after giving birth she'd decide what that part of her life was going to look like. That could take a few months she knew, especially since she'd never been good at keeping up with an exercise routine. Maybe she *should* consider a little fun while she could, something to tide her over. But the thought of going to bed with some random person only made her think of the one person who kept invading her erotic dreams, Viktor.

Martha just shrugged. "Well then, how about birthing classes, have you signed up yet?"

"I need to call today. It's on the list."

"And what about a partner for that? I wish I could go, I'd love to be your birthing coach but," she waved at her enormous belly.

"I am going to have my dad go with me." He'd already offered and since she didn't feel comfortable asking Viktor at this point, she was going to take him up on it.

"Chastity?"

Chastity turned, surprised to find Jason, the nice vampire who'd driven her away from the party standing by her table.

"Jason," she said with a half-smile, gaze darting around to make sure Viktor wasn't about to walk up behind him, she knew they were friends.

"You're the one who dropped her off at my house. You are friends with Viktor," Martha accused.

He held up his hands and bowed his head. "Yes, sorry, that was before. Now I just can't stand the guy." He lifted his gaze and winked at Chastity.

"Even I don't hate him," she said with a sigh because sometimes she wished she did. "Would you like to join us?"

"Actually I would, but let me order first."

Jason walked inside and Martha raised an eyebrow at Chastity.

"What?" Chastity demanded.

"He's cute."

"He's also Viktor's friend."

"So?"

"So, I'm not interested in him."

"Sure, sure. Ah," Martha growled and rubbed at her stomach.

"Are you alright?"

"Just a little contraction."

It didn't look little, and it wasn't the first one since they'd sat down to chat Chastity was sure, but this one was worse because Martha wasn't able to hide it quite so well. Chastity watched nervously as Martha huffed and rubbed her belly. When she finally stopped, she still moved uncomfortably in her chair.

"You look miserable, you should go home," Chastity said.

"I am, and I can't."

"Why?"

"Because no one else is available to work."

"You aren't working. You're sitting out here with me," Chastity argued.

"If Glen needs help, I'll go inside and help," she pouted then Martha groaned as another contraction hit and this time Glen stepped outside with a worried look on his face.

Chastity met his wide gaze. "Why don't you take her in to see her doctor, just for a quick check. I can stay and make coffee for a few hours."

"Just until Benjamin gets off school and shows up," Martha said with a grunt.

"Oh fun, I'll help," Jason offered, having followed Glen outside.

"Can you make coffee?" Chastity asked.

"Coffee, yes, but lattes and mochas, not so much."

"Well then, I'll be in charge of the drinks, and you can bag bagels. I worked at a coffee shop every summer in high school."

Glen gave some brief instructions then ushered his wife to the car.

Chastity looked at Jason who was pulling on a white apron and wished she wasn't pregnant with his friend's baby because he was so damn cute.

"Do I need a hair net?" he asked playfully.

"Only if you want to look ridiculous."

"It's my only goal in life," he said seriously, then tossed an apron to her.

Viktor stood outside Mooncalled and thought he must be having a nightmare. Inside the shop Jason and Chastity stood behind the counter in matching white aprons, chatting and laughing and serving customers.

When Jason reached out and tucked a lock of her hair behind her ear Viktor snapped out of his shock and stalked inside.

"Vik! Can I get you your usual?" Jason asked, grabbing a cup and tossing it into the air then catching it.

"What is all this?" Viktor asked, hoping he sounded casual but by the smug look on Jason's face, he doubted he had hit it.

"Martha might be in labor," Chastity explained.

"But it's too early." Viktor had been in often, and knew Martha was still a few weeks from her due date, which she was not happy about.

"It's probably nothing, but Glen took her in to get checked anyway."

"Luckily we were here to take over," Jason said cheerily.

"Yeah, lucky," Viktor hissed.

"I'll get your latte with cinnamon," Chastity said and turned.

Viktor was impressed she remembered his order and he glared at Jason as he paid.

"Oh shit, would you look at the time," Jason said suddenly. "I have a thing," he said and took off his apron, throwing it at Viktor with a meaningful look.

"You're leaving me here?" Chastity gasped.

"Yeah, sorry. I didn't think it would be this long, I have got to run."

Viktor knew his friend was lying, and he knew why. He wasn't going to let this opportunity fall out of his lap. "I'll stay and help, I know how to run a cash register, probably better than Jason."

"Oh, yeah I guess you probably do," Chastity said carefully, and handed him his finished drink.

Viktor went around the counter and got a good look at her. Even with the apron on, he could tell that she was starting to show a little and he had a near overwhelming urge to reach out and touch the evidence of his growing child. But he figured she would not appreciate the gesture so he fisted his hands and gritted his teeth.

Jason left with a wave, and no other customers were inside, so they were suddenly standing awkward and alone.

"You look good, how have you been feeling?" Viktor asked, breaking the silence when he couldn't take it any longer. She was wiping the counter over and over as far from him as possible. He hated that they were like this, especially since he'd experienced what it could be like when they were getting along, more than getting along, they had been almost dating before his father had fucked everything up so grandly.

She turned to face him but gripped the rag like it was going to save her life. "Definitely on the upswing, which I guess is what to expect at this point in the pregnancy."

"Second trimester high," he said with a nod.

"Yeah, uh, well it seems pretty slow now. Gosh it was crazy for Jason and I. Must be the afternoon slump, too early for pre-dinner coffee drinkers."

Viktor wasn't sure if she was hinting that he wasn't needed or what, but thankfully just then a whole group came in and they were busy for the next hour with a steady stream of customers.

Chastity really did know what she was doing behind the counter. She frothed milk and brewed coffee, mixed and sprinkled and every customer seemed satisfied with the results. He felt a little lame because he was only able to hand out food and take money, but it worked, they worked. They slid right into a comfortable rhythm that felt old instead of new. He wanted to tell her, point out that they were a great team, that they were obviously meant to handle things together. But he didn't, it wasn't the right place and he wasn't positive that it was the right time. Was she ready to talk? To possibly forgive and find a way that they could move on together?

The crowd had settled to just a few stragglers when Benjamin and one of his friends walked in and reported that his mom and dad were at home. The baby wasn't coming yet, which was a relief, but Martha was on bed rest.

Viktor and Chastity handed off their aprons and left the shop, but neither hurried away from the sidewalk. Viktor took that as a good sign and decided to take the first step toward reconciliation.

"Do you have dinner plans? I'd love to cook for you."

She looked surprised by his offer and a little unsure. "That would be alright, I am hungry," she said. It wasn't an ecstatic yes, but he'd take it.

The spike of joy that jolted through him at her words should have resulted from something more significant than a lackluster acceptance of dinner. But with her, he would take whatever he could get and build something more from there, if she let him.

As he followed her across the street his eyes roamed over her backside with appreciation. She was wearing stretchy shorts that showed him everything he wanted to caress, lick and spank.

"Fuck," he mumbled as his fangs descended and his cock hardened. He'd managed to keep his mind off of her body while they were working, but now they were just with each other in a social way and he couldn't stop thinking of all the things he would do to her...if this were a date.

CHAPTER TWENTY

Chastity wasn't sure why she'd said yes to Viktor's invitation, except that she really was hungry. She knew they needed to be on some kind of solid ground as well, it was best for the baby and it helped that it hadn't been unpleasant working with him at Mooncalled. In fact, she'd enjoyed it quite a bit, maybe too much. She had valiantly ignored the warmth that spread through her body every time he'd gotten close to her behind the counter. She knew it was just the hormones, but damn, why did he smell so fucking good? She couldn't deny that was at least part of the reason she'd accepted the invitation. A chance to stay close to him for longer, and to be in his home where his scent would surround her. She might orgasm just sitting on his couch. Could she explain it away as a weird pregnancy symptom?

They walked to his beach shop and house. She'd seen it before, of course, she'd spent time on this beach and walked past it many times in her life. But she'd never been inside the surf shop since she'd never been interested in surfing.

"This is nice," she said, taking in the small but clean and organized shop.

"Thank you, it does well. The shop plus the lessons. It's an added bonus that I live right upstairs so I'm on the beach. I grew up in the city and I joined this coven as soon as I could get out from under my father's thumb. All I ever wanted was a quiet life doing what I love."

Chastity latched onto his train of thought, wanting to know more about him and his father's relationship. "Did he resent that? You leaving the city for this simple existence?"

"Oh yeah, he had hoped I would follow in his political footsteps, but it was never an interest to me. I just want to live my life; simple and pleasurable. He gets a lot of sympathy for having a deadbeat son," he added with a grimace.

"I get that. A lot of people thought I was crazy to not do something more with my art degree. Like I needed to go get a job teaching or running a museum or something. To them, just staying home and painting seemed like not enough, but it is enough for me."

"And will it be enough for you and a child?" Viktor asked.

"Are you asking if I make enough money to support my child? Do you think I would be stupid enough to get pregnant if I wasn't?" she snapped.

"I—no—I just had to ask," he said with a shrug. "I know you've never said anything about needing financial assistance from me, and I do plan to support half of whatever the child needs."

Chastity pursed her lips and nodded. She didn't want to argue with him, and she did think it made sense he'd pay for stuff for the child. "What were you thinking of cooking?" she asked to change the subject.

His wary expression relaxed. "Follow me up and we'll see what I have. I think I can do some burgers."

She followed him back out of the shop and then up a staircase at the back of the building. A surprisingly cheery yellow door greeted them and when he opened it for her, she stepped into a small bright space that smelled like him. She had to swallow a groan as her body reacted. There were heavy curtains on the windows to keep out sunlight, but he'd made up for the lack with lamps in nearly every corner. His floor was a creamy wood, and the walls a soft blue making her think of clear skies. His furniture was bright orange mixed with pale yellow and the pictures on the walls featured scenes of ocean waves with surfers gliding through water. The living room flowed into a small kitchen with a bar for eating—no table. There was a small hallway off the living room that led back to what she assumed was the bedroom and bathroom.

It was a tight space but somehow still bright and cheery.

"You look surprised," he said with a laugh.

"I just always imagine vampires living in spaces a little more Dracula and a lot less beachy. Though I should have expected this, based on your choice in shirts and vehicle," she laughed. She walked around to investigate the space closer and gasped when she spotted a painting hanging in the hallway. It was an image of palm trees at sunrise with two lovers embracing in the sand beneath, just a hint of nudity in their twisting limbs.

"I found out the gallery down the beach sells some of your stuff and when I checked it out this one really spoke to me."

"It's one of my favorites," she agreed. "I hope they gave you a good deal."

"Definitely not, but I also didn't tell them the artist was pregnant with my child, maybe that would have helped."

"I doubt it, Bernard is a stickler for price, which is why I let him sell my stuff. Tourists pay a lot for local art to take home with them."

"It was worth it," he said, and she looked over in time to see a hint of red in his cheeks as he turned to the kitchen. "Let's see what I have to eat."

They had burgers, rare, and salad. Their conversations stayed neutral as they ate, mostly getting to know each other rather than talking about the baby or Viktor's father's horrible plan to use it for political gain.

She didn't want to leave without bringing up the article though so as he cleaned up the dishes she pulled it out of her purse. "Did you know about this?"

Viktor gave her a puzzled look and picked up the magazine. She could tell right away that he hadn't and she almost felt bad for considering he'd been in on it. Almost. In truth she didn't know him well enough to say if he'd be that sort of sneaky. She wanted to believe the best of him, but she worried that her libido was blinding her to his motives.

"I wish I could say that I can't believe he did this, but it is very much on brand for him."

She nodded, willing to take his word for it.

When Chastity left, Viktor walked her to her car and it felt like the end of a date. Chastity couldn't stop looking at his mouth and licking her own lips in anticipation.

She dropped her gaze to her keys. "I guess I'll see you later, I um, don't have another appointment for a while but I do have to sign up for some birthing classes."

"I want to attend," he said quickly.

She met his eyes which were wide with hope. "Okay, I'll pick one and let you know when it is."

"Thank you, Chastity."

She nodded and got in her car before she could embarrass herself by staring at his mouth again like a desperate hussy. On the drive home she couldn't help thinking about how nice it had been to spend time with Viktor, how easy he was to be around, and how, if she'd met him in any other scenario, she would have really enjoyed dating him.

. . .

Viktor sat on his couch sipping a beer after Chastity left. He was trying to convince himself that she hadn't been looking at his lips quite as much as he thought, and she certainly hadn't been licking her own lips while doing so. He shifted on the couch uncomfortably as his cock argued with him and something hard prodded at his back. He reached his hand into the cushion and pulled out Chastity's cellphone.

That wasn't good. He didn't like the idea of her being home alone with no way to contact anyone in case of an emergency. He headed out to his van before he could think too much about his real reasons. She wouldn't mind him dropping by with it, he was sure, even if it was a little late, it wasn't quite an indecent hour yet.

As he drove to her house he kept thinking about the last time he'd been there and how defeated he'd felt. How hopeless it had all seemed and how sure he'd been that he'd missed his chance to be more than just a resented part-time father in her life. But today had been pleasant, if a little strained, and he had renewed hope that they would be able to forge a friendship of sorts and raise the child happily.

Then his mind slipped farther back to when he'd kissed her, when he'd pulled away only because he didn't want to create awkwardness that would affect the way they raised their child. But he had really wanted to see where that kiss would lead, and it had featured in every one of his fantasies since. Along with the images he'd seen during that accidental video call.

Just thinking about *that* made his shorts tighten and when he parked outside her house, the stiffness in his cock and the racing of his heartbeat were the only excuse he had for overlooking the fact that all of her lights were off so she was obviously already in bed. It didn't occur to him though until he was standing on her porch and he'd finally convinced his cock back down and his fangs back in.

"Shit," he mumbled and took a closer look at the house realizing his mistake. He was already there though, and he had her phone in hand. He didn't want her to be without it, he also didn't want to wake her up. He knocked softly. If she was awake, she'd hear it and if she was asleep it wouldn't disturb her. There was no answer and no noise from inside. He decided his best option was to slip in and just leave it. It wouldn't be the first time he'd snuck in.

Like a true creature of the night, he slipped through the shadows to the window of her garage studio which he knew she left open to vent the paint fumes.

It didn't take much for him to pull his body up to the high window and snake through. When he landed on the floor he froze for a moment, waiting to hear her run through the house in alarm at the obvious intruder. When no sound came, he tiptoed through the messy studio.

He stopped in front of a canvas set up on an easel, the paint looked damp as if she'd added a bit just before she'd gone to bed. It was all black with silver and gold minimalistic swipes that indicated the form of a pregnant woman. Her head was back and face pointed up. It was beautiful in its simplicity, and he wanted it, he wanted to hang it in his bedroom and stare at it constantly. He reached out and almost touched it but pulled back just before contact, afraid of messing up her artistry.

She really was talented. His sister was right, she'd have been a great match for him as a girlfriend, if she wasn't already pregnant with his child.

Moving on, he snuck through the door leading into her living room where he planned to leave the phone as if she'd dropped it. She'd never know that he had been there.

A moan coming from the bedroom stopped him dead in his tracks.

Was she with someone?

Possessive rage filled him.

Before he could tell himself it was a terrible idea, he took long strides toward her bedroom and the sounds of her pleasure.

He shoved open the door ready to commit all kinds of atrocities with no care for the consequences that would come.

The sight that met him stopped him in his tracks and held him in thrall. His mouth hung open and his body switched from fight to fuck instantly. His fangs sprang out with unending need.

CHAPTER TWENTY-ONE

Chastity had been too worked up to sleep after her dinner with Viktor. She'd gone into her studio and painted a little, then she tried tea. Nothing worked and so she'd reached for her battery-operated wand, one that Martha had insisted she was going to need in the coming months. It had a long reach, and she would be able to get around her ever-growing belly with it to hit the spot she liked.

It hadn't taken long for the magical vibrations to fill her with warmth. Soon she was letting out her pleasure in unabashed moans while envisioning Viktor, because she just couldn't help herself.

Then he was standing there in her bedroom doorway as if conjured by her dirty thoughts. She screamed, pulling the blanket up over her spread legs, her naked bottom half, and that damn vibrator.

"What the fuck are you doing in here?" she demanded when he just stood there unmoving, red eyes glued to the spot where the blankets continued to buzz and move.

"Phone," he said, holding up what she assumed was her phone that she'd left behind at his house. She had realized she'd left it but had figured she would swing by tomorrow and grab it, no big deal. Never in her wildest imaginings would she have pictured him breaking into her house to deliver it to her bedroom.

"Okay, now get the fuck out of here," she snarled.

His gaze shot to her face then and he seemed to snap out of the trance he'd been in. "Oh my god, Chastity, I—I need some blood," he said then turned and walked away.

She listened to him make his way down the hall but she was surprised to not hear the front door open and close. Instead she heard the distinct sounds of him rummaging around her refrigerator. She didn't have any blood, so she expected to hear him leave quickly. The mood ruined, she turned off the vibrator and yanked on her shorts ready to go lock the door behind him.

Then she heard the pop of frying eggs.

"What the hell?" she grumbled and threw on a robe. She knew she needed to confront his erratic behavior but she wanted to be well covered before she did.

"Hungry?" he asked as she leaned against the kitchen doorframe, arms crossed over her chest.

"What do you think you're doing?"

"You don't have any blood so I'm making eggs with the blood seasoning."

"Why?" she demanded.

He stiffened and took a breath, his torso shaking. "I can't leave," he said so quiet she wasn't sure she'd heard him right.

"I'm certain you can. You don't live here, and I didn't even invite you in." She turned and looked at the front door, still deadbolted. "How did you get in?"

"Garage window."

"Okay, well, you're welcome to use the front door to leave."

He turned and faced her then. His eyes were bright red and the fangs she'd known were slurring his words protruded from his mouth farther than she'd ever seen. She couldn't help taking a step back, this was a monster in her kitchen.

"I won't hurt you," he said and there was pain in his face, a pleading wrinkle to his brow. "I just need to get myself under control before I leave here."

She thought she understood then. He was nearing a blood frenzy. It was when a vampire became so driven by their lust for blood they couldn't control who they might harm. But why had he come here if he'd known he was that hungry? In fact, she'd seen him sip blood while they were together earlier, so she knew he wasn't starved. It took vampires abstaining from blood for a month at least for them to enter into the kind of craze he seemed on the edge of.

"What's going on?" she demanded.

"I want you."

"You want my blood? I thought being pregnant with your baby would be a deterrent." She wasn't sure why she thought that, but it had seemed reasonable.

Viktor shook his head. "It's not, trust me. In fact, it makes it more desirable, makes me want to claim you hard and fast and thoroughly. But it's not just about your blood, Chastity, it's also about your perfect body and walking in to see you—" he groaned, "I am going to lose it if I don't satisfy at least one urge as soon as possible."

Her eyes drifted down to the obvious bulge in his shorts and she bit her lip. "Oh," was all she could manage to say as her thighs clenched and a swirl of desire spiraled through her. She wanted to offer to help with that urge he was dealing with. She wanted to be wanton and spontaneous, but she was also slightly terrified of the bloodthirsty look in his eye.

Viktor made a pained noise as if he knew what she was thinking and turned back to the eggs—which were now looking well done—and dumped all that remained in the bottle of blood spice on top of them.

Chastity didn't trust her lusty thoughts, so she kept her mouth shut as she watched. He put the eggs on two plates then set them at the table indicating for her to join him. She wasn't sure if it was safe or not, but she knew that she wanted to eat that food, it smelled amazing.

"Should we talk about this?" she asked carefully as she sat.

"When we're done eating," he said, mouth still full of fang.

Chastity trusted that he knew what he was doing, so she ate, and watched him eat. He had his eyes half closed staring down at his food so she felt free to stare. Every time he put a bite in his mouth his eyes closed all the way and he made a sound of enjoyment that sent a thrill through her body. When he licked a bit of food from his lips she peeked at his fangs that were a little less prominent now. It was the most erotic thing she had ever seen in her entire life.

By the time he was done eating she was wet between her thighs, her nipples were hard, and she was thinking longingly about the vibrator in her bedroom. Maybe the mood hadn't been completely ruined.

Viktor set down his fork and finally lifted his gaze to her. His eyes were back to red-brown but a little on the darker side than they normally were, and she thought his fangs must be completely retracted now because of the shape of his lips. There was nothing to fear in this face and she realized she'd had nothing to fear before either. He had no desire to harm her or anyone else. He was just a horny vampire, and she was his current object of desire.

"I realize that I made a miscalculation when I came in to return your phone. I didn't think clearly when I heard your sounds of pleasure, and honestly, I don't know what I would have done if I'd found you in bed with someone."

He flicked his gaze away briefly, guilt on his features.

"I appreciate you driving out here to return my phone," she said, because she wasn't sure what to say about the rest.

"I did knock first, but you must not have heard me," he defended then shook his head. "Never mind, that isn't what is important here. What we need to discuss is my reaction to what I saw in there. I don't want you to be afraid of me."

"I'm not," she said, maybe a little too quickly because he quirked up one side of his lips in a doubtful smirk. "I know you don't want to harm me. I am pregnant with your child."

"If it was only that, then I wouldn't have had such a strong reaction. The truth is, Chastity, I am very much attracted to you."

"Oh." She wasn't sure how to respond, she was attracted to him too, but that didn't change the awkward situation they were in.

"Would you ever consider me, Chastity? As more than a father to your child?" His voice was high as if he were straining to control the emotions behind the question, afraid to hope that she wouldn't reject him.

"I don't know," she answered honestly. The look of defeat on his face had Chastity instantly regretting her answer but she wanted to be completely honest with him. "What if we take it slow?" she added.

His eyes widened and he took in a sharp breath. "Like dating?"

"I know it seems a little silly since we're already having a baby together, but we haven't been intimate or anything. It seems reasonable to see if we like each other in a dating scenario."

"Very reasonable," he agreed with an eager lilt to his voice.

"So no more sneaking into my house," she said with a frown.

"I think I can agree to that, but I warn you, if I ever think you're in danger I will knock down any door, climb through any window, to get to you."

His words made her heart flutter the same way all those morally grey men's proclamations in romance novels did. "And your father stays out of it."

"You'll get no argument from me on that one."

Chastity smiled, this felt good. "Okay then, I think we have a deal. I am tired and full and ready to get back to bed now though."

"Back to bed ... or back to your not so little friend in there?" he teased, and her cheeks flared.

"Wouldn't you like to know," she teased back. "Now out."

"Fine, but I am taking you out tomorrow, how about lunch?"

"I'm spending most of the day with Martha. I promised to keep the little kids out of the way so Glen can work the shop and she gets the bed rest she needs."

"I'll help you babysit then, pick you up in the morning."

"Okay."

He smiled brightly and stood, taking her plate and his to the sink.

"I'll get those in the morning, you should head home."

He looked like he wanted to argue but finally relented, just wiping the counter quickly and making sure the dishes were rinsed.

Chastity walked him to the door thinking that she might want to consider getting him an emergency key so she didn't risk any broken windows or doors in the future. He turned to her in the doorway and pulled her to him, his hot body felt so good pressed against her that she nearly groaned. Then he pressed his mouth to hers and kissed her soft and slow. It was brief and there was no tongue, but it was filled with promises of so much more. When he walked out the door, she watched him go with a smile on her face that she just knew Martha would call *dopey*.

She really needed that vibrator now.

Viktor left Chastity's house with a new spring in his step and anxious hope in his heart. He was unexpectedly drawn to her, had been since he'd first seen her and her little birthmark on the beach. Her being pregnant with his child added to the appeal, but it wasn't the only reason he was attracted to her and that attraction was only growing as he got to know her.

He wasn't afraid to admit that he liked the way pregnancy was filling out her curves, and knowing that she had a piece of himself inside her had his instincts going into overdrive to claim and protect her. He couldn't imagine feeling this same way about a married vampire who he had signed a contract with to bear his child like originally intended.

With Chastity, he wanted so much more. He wanted to be there for everything, and that should have scared him. But it only thrilled him because she was going to give him a chance. She was going to let him prove that he could be a father, a boyfriend, a lover maybe. He couldn't wait.

His phone rang and he frowned down at his father's number. He'd been avoiding the man's phone call for weeks, but he knew he couldn't avoid it forever.

He hit the button to answer the video call and leaned over the hood of his van. "Hello, father." Johnson Paulie was sitting in a leather chair in his home office with one of his current secretaries slash girlfriends standing behind him in an almost see-through white top. She was far too young for him but that's what his father preferred and he often flaunted it in front of his son in an attempt to prove his lifestyle was something to be desired. *Your young vampire looks will fade with the sun, boy. You need a career that will keep you in the style I know you so enjoy long into old age*, he'd often told Viktor.

"How's my grandchild? Do we know if it's a boy or a girl? A boy would be my preference, but a girl would gain me a sort of sympathy I'm missing from female voters."

Viktor's grip on his phone tightened and his jaw clenched. "I don't know," he hissed. "But Chastity is healthy and so is the baby, that's all I care about."

"Sure, son, but you need to get her to sign that agreement."

Viktor was at the end of what he could take from this asshole.

"No," he hissed. "*You* need to get her to sign that agreement. I need to be a father to the child and protect them both from people who would use them for personal gain."

Johnson's eyes narrowed at his son through the phone and he leaned forward on his desk, trying to intimidate as if they were in the same room together. "Bah, babies don't need fathers and they are only good for what they can help us to gain until they're old enough to become a disappointment," he snapped back.

"I guess you would think so," Viktor said with a shake of his head, all fight gone from his body, it was the same old story with his father and he was so tired of playing into his games. He hung up without another word.

"Oh, Viktor," Chastity said from behind him, her voice strained with emotion.

Viktor spun around and saw Chastity standing there with her arms wrapped tightly around herself and a look of sympathy on her face.

He wasn't sure what she'd heard, but he feared the worst. "I'm not going to ask you to sign anything," he assured her.

"I know," she said quietly and took a step toward him. "The rumors are true, aren't they?"

He watched her warily. "Depends on which ones you're referring to."

Chastity closed the distance between them and reached up to grasp his face. She looked so deep into his eyes he thought she must be seeing his soul.

"Your father, he was never there for you or Persia was he? Your mother died when you were young and you two were raised mostly by the help."

"Just a couple of unfortunate rich kids, yeah, I know. I've heard it all my life," Viktor tried to brush off her concern, but he also wanted to let her wrap him in her comforting warmth.

"I'm sorry," she whispered and pulled him down to kiss his lips lightly.

He put his arms around her and deepened the kiss. Her body was hot against his and she shivered as his tongue stroked along her lip. His body reacted to her, his cock thickening and his fangs descending.

He pulled back and grunted "Shit, sorry."

She blinked up at him, desire making her face flush and her eyes bright. "For what?"

"My reaction to you. You were just offering me comfort and I am about to molest you," he said with a laugh, but it was true. All he could think about was picking her up and turning around so he could fuck her against the side of his van.

"Maybe I don't mind," she said, pushing her hips forward.

Viktor groaned. "I thought we were going to take things slow."

"Too late, I'm already pregnant," she said pressing a kiss to his neck.

"Did you follow me out here because you want me in your bed, Chastity?"

"No, I followed you out because you left your jacket."

Viktor put a little distance between them and realized she had his coat on. Then he realized that she was trying to sleep with him out of sympathy for his crappy childhood. And that was more than enough to cool his desire. He slid the coat off her arms and she shivered, making him regret that he was going to be strong for them both right now and say goodnight.

"I'll see you tomorrow for babysitting duty." He gave her a chaste kiss then walked around the van.

Chastity stepped back and watched him drive away.

"I'm an idiot, or I'm finally understanding what it means to care about the person I want to sleep with," Viktor grumbled as he watched her get smaller and smaller in his rearview mirror. "Maybe both."

CHAPTER TWENTY-TWO

The next morning, as promised, Viktor picked Chastity up to go babysit Martha's kids. He looked a little nervous as he handed her a bag. "It's more of the blood spice and a couple blood bags, I hope you don't mind. It's just in case I am here and I need it again, more efficient than cooking."

"Oh," she said, her own cheeks reddening as she hurried into the kitchen. He wanted to be prepared to be turned on in her house again. The feelings that evoked in her were conflicting. A part of her was glad he thought it would happen again and was preparing to efficiently keep her safe, the other part, a dark and curious part, was sad that he wasn't going to jump on her and tear into her at the next opportunity.

"I did some research on birthing classes." Viktor said. "It looks like there are a lot of different options. Have you thought about what you're looking for?"

Chastity turned from closing the fridge to see him hovering just inside the kitchen, still looking like he wasn't quite sure he should be there.

"I've looked but haven't picked yet. I'm really glad you're going to help me today."

He gave her a bright smile. "I hope Martha feels the same way. She's been glaring at me every time I walk into Mooncalled over the last month. Did you warn her I'm tagging along?"

"Yeah, I told her she can chill on that for now, sorry, she's just trying to be a supportive friend."

He shrugged, obviously not that worried about it. "Werewolves are like that. Fiercely loyal to those they include in their pack. I expected it, but I kept going back because I wanted her to know that I wasn't going to be scared off that easily. And I was hoping to run into you," he admitted.

"Why?" Chastity couldn't help asking. "Why didn't you just stop trying? You didn't ask for this, this isn't what you ever wanted." She looked down at her hands, unable to meet his gaze as she confessed her worries. "Why are you still trying to be in my life after I shut you out?"

"I may not have been after this sort of situation at the start, Chastity, but I am now. Now I want this."

Chastity lifted her gaze to meet his and her heart started racing. What exactly was he saying?

"I want to be as much a part of the pregnancy and child's life as you'll let me. I hadn't planned to be more than an occasional father, that's true, but now I want to be as much of a father as I can be. Besides, the kid will need a lot of vampire help and I should be the one to give it that."

Chastity turned to hide her disappointment. He wanted to be here for the child, not her. What had she expected though? No kiss, no accidental flashing, and no walking in on her masturbating was going to change that. She needed to stop letting her fantasies run in that direction.

Chastity wiped down the already spotless counters as she gathered her emotions back up. When she turned back to Viktor he had a curious look on his face she couldn't decipher.

"Ready," she said and strode past him to grab her purse with her head held high. He didn't want her, and she was not going to let him know she wished for anything else.

As soon as Chastity walked into Martha's bedroom, the werewolf started in on questioning and Chastity was glad to tell her everything.

"Wow, so you think he just wants to be a really good dad?"

"I do, which is great. That's the best I could hope for in this situation, right?" Why couldn't she just be happy about that?

Martha made a noncommittal noise in her throat.

Chastity walked to the window and looked out at Viktor playing with the twins in the yard. It looked like some sort of game where they shot him with foam darts and he pretended to disintegrate like a vampire in an old movie.

"He's good with kids. His niece absolutely adores him, and he's not wrong. I am not going to be able to teach our child about the vampire stuff."

"I think that's the first time you referred to it as 'our' child instead of just 'my' child. You're accepting him."

Chastity turned back to her friend and bit her lip. "Do you think that's stupid? After what his father tried to pull?"

"No, I think it's good. Viktor doesn't seem to care what his father's wishes are, so you have to admit he's already being rightfully protective. I think he wants to be involved for the right reasons."

"I guess maybe that means it will be easier for me to date if we do shared custody of some kind. If I can trust him to take care of the baby, then it will give me a little more freedom." That had never been part of her plan and even as she said it a piece of her heart broke. She couldn't imagine being mandated to leave her child with anyone, even Viktor.

"Oh yeah, I'm sure he'll be willing to babysit so you can go out with some random guy," Martha scoffed. "That man is going to want to own your soul, Chastity, I can smell it on him. He's possessive of you."

"That's just because I'm pregnant. That will all change when I have the baby and we are two separate entities. And then he can't expect me to stay celibate," she snapped back.

Martha nodded but Chastity didn't feel like the woman was actually agreeing with her.

"When is Elaine getting back?" Chastity asked to change the subject.

"Tonight. She isn't hurrying because she said the Moon Goddess told her the baby isn't going to come early."

"Well that's good news, right?"

"Oh sure. But it also means I'll be stuck in bed that long and I am going to go insane."

Chastity sympathized but there was nothing she could do but offer to be a distraction for her friend.

Viktor was exhausted by the time he was driving Chastity back to her place, but he didn't want their time together to end.

"Can I make you dinner?"

"Okay," she agreed, and his heart sang at that one word. Every time she let him in, it made him greedy for more, always more of her. The realization had snuck up on him that there would never be enough, he wanted all of her, all day, every day.

But would she ever want him the same way? He was afraid to ask and be denied, so he would just insert himself as much as possible until she told him to stop.

Okay, that might be the wrong metaphor to think of because now the part of himself that he really wanted to insert into her was tingling. He grunted and shifted in his seat as he drove to her place.

He made her dinner and they chatted about birthing class options. He didn't give his opinion, but listened with interest as she talked about what she liked and disliked about each one. He knew that he wasn't in the position to make any demands about the way she brought this child into the world. Even if they'd been married he wouldn't have. It was her body going through this, his only job was to support her in the way she wanted.

After dinner they settled into the living room and Chastity pulled up the class schedules on her laptop. "It looks like there's a class once a week for six weeks starting tomorrow night, and they have an opening," Chastity said excitedly.

"The natural birthing class?"

"Yeah, they specialize in hospital births that are as natural as possible. I think that's what I'm looking for."

He nodded eagerly. "I can make that work." He mentally ran through his schedule, he'd have to cancel some lessons, but he didn't care. All that mattered was Chastity and the baby.

"Great, I'll register for it. If something comes up and you can't make one, my father will go with me, he was already planning to anyway."

"I'll be there," he said firmly, and she looked up from the screen, meeting his eyes. "I want to be there," he assured her.

She smiled at him and he felt like he'd won the lottery. Then she yawned and he frowned.

"You need to sleep."

"It's been a long day," she agreed and shut the laptop.

"Can I make you some tea?"

"No, I think I'm just going to shower and fall into bed."

He tried not to imagine her in the shower, but his body reacted anyway, his cock twitched and so did his fangs. "Well then, I'll pick you up tomorrow for more babysitting?"

"Actually, Martha's mom, Elaine, is coming back tonight. She was on some kind of goddess retreat, so there will be help. Sorry I forgot to mention that."

"No big deal. Then just for the birthing class?"

She nodded and followed him to the door. He didn't resist the urge to pull her in for a hug. "Sleep well," he whispered against her head, then left the house before he was overwhelmed with the desire to turn the goodbye hug into a lingering kiss.

CHAPTER TWENTY-THREE

Chastity spent the entire next day thinking about Viktor. He wasn't what she'd expected him to be after their first few dramatic interactions. He wasn't an intimidating selfish vampire, he wasn't a lazy beach bum, and he wasn't trying to be a part time father.

She didn't know how to deal with that when her feelings continued to rear up, her desire continued to wash through her when he smiled, and every damn time he did something even close to taking care of her she wanted to swoon. She was afraid to explore those feelings with him though. The baby was more important than her libido and if they slept together and made things awkward, that would just make things difficult for them raising a child together. Somehow the thought of her baby's daddy being her ex was way worse than her baby's father being a surprise sperm donor.

But if they slept together and continued sleeping together, if they lived together and—

Ugh, she needed to stop daydreaming about the father of her child, it wasn't healthy. They weren't going to get married and live happily ever after.

By the time Viktor showed up to take her to the birthing class she had almost canceled on him twice. She just wasn't sure how much of his attention she could take and still keep her feelings out of it. But as soon as she saw him standing on her porch, a look of excitement on his face, she melted all over again and was so thankful he was there. She wanted to always see his face like that, so different from what she'd seen when he first showed up at her house, scowling and angry because she'd been given his sperm. She might get hurt, she knew, but what if she didn't?

"Ready?" he asked.

"I think so. They said to bring a pillow, yoga mat, and water bottle." She held up the bag she'd packed. She was wearing comfortable clothes, as had been indicated. A pair of spandex shorts and a loose t-shirt. It didn't hide her slightly rounded belly and she caught Viktor looking at it with interest. He'd dressed casually athletic in basketball shorts and a cotton tank top. He looked good, as always, and she had to fight to keep from sweeping her gaze up and down his body. She knew her eyes would want to linger on places that she was extra curious about, places that might be highlighted in the fabric of those shorts.

"Sounds like we'll be having an interesting time," he laughed and took the bag from her.

When they walked into the large gymnasium at the rec center there were happy couples all around. Most of the women were obviously farther along than she was, with bulging bellies and all had adoring partners touching them, kissing them, and laughing with them.

Chastity felt like a fraud. She wanted to tell Viktor to forget it, this wasn't the right class for them. Maybe she needed to do a search for classes catering to humans who had been accidentally artificially inseminated by a vampire.

"Welcome, you must be Chastity and Viktor," an older woman said warmly as she walked up to them. "Find a space and set up, we'll begin shortly."

Viktor took the lead, and with a hand to Chastity's back he pushed her forward to a spot between a werewolf couple and a human one.

"Hey, is this your first time?" The young werewolf mother asked. She had a belly almost as large as Martha's and her husband kept rubbing it while she leaned back between his legs. It was intimate and Chastity couldn't hold the woman's gaze so she busied herself laying out their yoga mat as she answered affirmatively.

"Well, you'll love Jenna, she's a great teacher. We did the full class with our first and this time just thought we'd do a couple week refresher. I'm due soon so we won't make the full six classes."

"That's a great review, I'm glad we picked this one," Viktor said happily as he sat on the mat with his legs spread and his knees up like the other partners around the room. His shorts had fallen a bit up his thighs and the skin that was revealed had her licking her lips. It was paler than the rest of him and gave her a very good idea of what color his delicious ass would be. She chastised herself and forced her gaze back up, but she couldn't meet his eyes, so she stared at his forehead.

"I think you're supposed to sit," Viktor whispered.

The pillow was behind his back and Chastity bit her lip as she stared down at his waiting crotch. She looked desperately around the room. It was true. No one was standing except the teacher and no one was sitting in any other position. She sat in front of him, not allowing her body to touch his. She still felt the heat of his body behind her though, the promise of an embrace if she dared to lean back and settle against him like every other pregnant mother in the room was doing.

"Lean into your partners ladies, let him support you," Jenna said. "Let's start with some simple breathing exercises. Close your eyes and visualize your happy place. Let your partner's arms embrace your body as it grows your child."

Chastity didn't move. This was definitely a mistake. Who knew birthing classes would be such intimate affairs?

"Chastity, I think you need to lean against me," Viktor whispered.

She wanted to snap at him, tell him to stop telling her what she was supposed to do. But then Jenna walked over and raised an eyebrow at her, and Chastity leaned back, but she didn't scoot her ass toward him.

"No, no, let his thighs cradle your backside," Jenna said. "Otherwise you'll end up with a sore lower back, especially as the baby grows heavier."

Viktor grabbed her hips and pulled her tight against him. Chastity let out a little yelp.

"That's it," Jenna praised. "He is the partner, let him support you properly. That's why he's here," Jenna added with a smile then moved around the room checking other couples' positions.

"Relax," Viktor said against her ear, making her shiver. His arms moved up and down her arms. "I've got you, Chastity. Close your eyes, breathe, and think of your happy place."

Right now her happy place would be in bed in a very similar position as this but with a lot less clothing and no other couples nearby.

Her nipples hardened at the thought, and as she melted into him, she was pretty sure she heard Viktor groan behind her.

Thankfully Jenna started talking then, guiding them all through some simple breathing exercises and ending the fantasy Chastity had created in her mind.

The whole experience was much more hands on than she'd expected, as in Viktor's hands on her. By the time the class was done she was chugging water to try and cool her desire, and Viktor looked a little strained as well.

"So, what do you think? Jenna's amazing, isn't she?" the werewolf woman asked as her partner rolled their yoga mat.

"Oh yeah, it wasn't what I was expecting," Chastity admitted.

"But then again, this is my first time so I didn't know what to expect."

The woman laughed. "I hope to see you next week."

"What did you think?" Jenna asked, coming up to them.

"I think this is exactly what we wanted," Viktor answered for her.

"I'm so glad to hear that," Jenna said then walked off to check in with other couples.

Viktor had everything in hand except the water bottle Chastity was clutching like a lifeline, so they headed out. She wasn't sure she ever wanted to come back, despite Viktor's enthusiasm. As they walked out the front door Viktor's hand was on her back as if it was the most normal thing to be touching her. She supposed after what they'd just been through the small touch didn't seem like that big a deal, but it *was* different for them, more familiar and casual than they had been only hours before. He was standing closer to her than usual too, as if he didn't want to end the intimacy they'd just had. She didn't want it to end either.

A flash of light had them freezing.

"Woah, looks like my sources were correct. Viktor Paulie got a human pregnant."

The violent hiss that came from Viktor as he shoved her behind him was something Chastity had never heard before, and if it had been directed at her she would have probably peed her pants in fright.

"You'll regret selling those," Viktor snarled at the man.

"What's her name?" he called as Viktor tried to shield her and the man took more pictures.

"Viktor what's happening?" Chastity asked as she clung to the back of his shirt. Other people were leaving around them and they all looked on curiously, no doubt wondering what kind of spectacle they were witnessing.

"Keep your head down," he snapped at her and pulled her to

his side. He shielded her as best he could as he led her to his van, then shoved her in the back seat. As he ran around to the driver side the man continued to snap pictures of him and the van.

When they were out of the parking lot Chastity pulled herself from her stunned silence. "What the hell?" she demanded.

"I'm guessing this is a result of that article. My father doesn't care that he's forcing you into the spotlight."

Chastity was sure he was right, and it had been exactly what she'd feared when she saw the article. But she had reasoned that all of this would eventually come out one way or another. "Are you ashamed of me?" she asked, her voice choked with emotion.

Viktor slammed on the brakes and pulled to the side of the road. He flipped his body around to face her in the back. "How could you think that?"

"You shoved me around like a dirty secret, Viktor," she said, more hurt in her voice than she would have liked to reveal.

"No," he gasped. "I was trying to protect you. Do you have any idea what will happen once the national media gets wind of this?"

"Too late, obviously."

"No, I will find out who that guy works for and I will pay anything, I will threaten if I have to," he said darkly. "And I will shut my father down once and for all."

Chastity pursed her lips and shook her head. Her emotions were all over the place and her eyes stung with tears. She wasn't a dirty secret and neither was her child. There was no way to hide this forever and if Viktor thought he could, then he was either delusional or not in this fully like he claimed to be.

"That is not a good plan, and it's not worth the risk of jailtime for threatening people. I refuse to be hidden away. If you want to stay separate from us, then do that. But don't you dare stand on my porch begging to be let in then shove me behind you when anyone else is looking." She met his gaze and let him see her pain and determination.

"I—I—I just want to protect you," he said again, quieter this time.

"Protect me, or hide me?" she demanded.

"It's the same thing," he argued but there wasn't much behind it, she could tell he was rethinking his actions.

"No, it's not." She shook her head and sighed. "Just take me home." She turned to look out the window, arms crossed over her belly in a protective gesture.

Viktor hesitated as if he wanted to keep talking about this, keep defending his actions, but he eventually started driving again. When she was sure he wasn't paying attention to her, a tear slipped out no matter how hard she was trying to hold it back.

She didn't acknowledge him when they got to her place, just grabbed her bag and hurried to her door, closing and locking it behind her in case he hadn't gotten the hint that she was not interested in any more conversation tonight.

She knew it was contrary and probably made her half-crazy but she was disappointed when no knocking came, no phone call or text to demand they talk. Just the sound of him driving away.

He was willing to fight to keep her and the baby a secret, but he wasn't willing to fight to talk to her about how it all made her feel and that hurt, a lot. She threw herself down on her bed and bawled until she fell asleep.

Viktor drove straight to his father's place in the city. He ignored the butler's demands that he wait to be announced, and shoved into his father's office where the man was sitting behind his desk with a cup of blood in one hand and a cigar in the other.

"Viktor, so nice to see you, son. Have you come with news of the child? Is it a boy or a girl?"

Viktor bared his fangs at his father. "You tipped off the press.

And how the hell did you even know we were going to be at that class? Were you having me followed, or Chastity?"

Johnson looked utterly unsurprised by his son's accusations, just took a sip of his blood and set his cigar down.

"I gave you both time to make a choice, but elections are drumming up and I need the press sooner rather than later. It seems I have an actual contender for my seat, a werewolf woman," Johnson scoffed. "As if she has a chance."

Viktor didn't comment on the obvious fact that if his father truly believed the woman didn't have a chance then he wouldn't be worried, that kind of logic never got through his father's thick skull. "My child is not a tool for reelection, and if you ever want to set eyes on it, you had better stop that story from running," Viktor threatened and turned to leave.

"You care for the girl," Johnson accused.

Viktor stopped but he didn't turn around. "I know it seems like a foreign concept to you, father, but I care for the woman who will birth my child, *and* I care for my child. Both far too much to let you use them for your political gain."

That shut him up and Viktor smiled as he walked out of the office and house. He knew that no matter what he said his father wasn't likely to understand what Viktor wanted and why. He had used Viktor and Persia when they were children for staged photo opportunities and examples of how a good vampire was raised. He didn't ever bother with them outside of those goals though, and so the threat to not see his grandchild wasn't going to be enough. Viktor needed to get ahead of the story.

He pulled out his phone and called Sara.

CHAPTER TWENTY-FOUR

Chastity woke up to the sounds of knocking. It wasn't the familiar tones of Viktor, but a more polite soft knock. She threw a robe over her pajamas that she'd put on sometime in the middle of the night when she'd woken up from her cry-induced sleep and rubbed at her face which was still crusty from salty tears. She padded to the front door expecting a delivery of paint she'd ordered. When she opened it, she wanted to cry all over again.

It was the beautiful vampire from the party, the one that Viktor had gone off with when Johnson had tricked her outside. The one that Viktor supposedly wasn't sleeping with but his father definitely would like him to be, and she looked fucking gorgeous despite the early hour. She was dressed in a tight black dress that hit her mid-thigh, and heels that accentuated her long pale legs. She looked like a model with her black hair swept up in a stylish ponytail and delicate pearls in her ears. She took off her dark sunglasses to reveal dark eyes a shade redder than Viktor's making her look fierce and perhaps hungry. Her ruby red lips twisted into a smirk as Chastity just gaped at her.

"Hey babe, I'm here to save the day. I'm Sara. We didn't get to meet the other night but I saw you across the room and my brother has told me about you."

"Excuse me?" Chastity managed to mumble, not sure if this was a nightmare or reality.

"My brother, Jason, gave you a ride home from the party."

Chastity nodded, she could see the resemblance there.

"Viktor called and said, and I quote *No one can do what you do so well, Sara.*" She smirked. "So here I am, let me in and we'll talk."

Chastity stepped aside so the woman could enter the house, but she still didn't understand what was going on. She went to the kitchen while Sara wandered around the house looking at things and making little noises that Chastity was sure meant she found everything here *cute* and *fun* for a human and all, but certainly not up to her standards as a wealthy vampire.

Chastity made two cups of peppermint tea and handed one to Sara who had wandered into her studio and was eyeing her half-finished work thoughtfully.

"You're good."

"Thanks," Chastity said, not sure if she should be offended by the level of surprise in the woman's tone. "Why exactly are you here?"

"Like I said, Viktor called me in to do damage control."

"What damage?"

"Oh honey, your picture is all over the tabloids today. You are on the lips of every vampire and politician in the country."

"Shit," she mumbled, remembering the photographer last night.

"Yeah, shit."

"I guess Viktor's pretty pissed that people learned he's going to be having a baby with a human?"

Sara tilted her head and eyed Chastity. "Something like that."

"And you're here because ..." Chastity prompted.

"I'm a PR genius."

"Damage control." Chastity didn't like the sound of that.

"Exactly. So we need to talk before Viktor gets here." She looked suddenly quite serious. "I need to know what you are hoping to get out of this whole thing before we decide on what avenue to take."

"What do you mean? I'm not getting anything, other than the baby that I went to the fertility clinic to conceive. The father was a surprise, as I'm sure you already know."

"Right, but now, what do you want *now*?"

Chastity had a feeling it was a loaded question, and she was far too sleep deprived to understand the ramifications of answering. "I want a healthy baby, it's all I ever wanted," she said quietly, ignoring the stab in her gut at the loss of Viktor, someone she never had and should have known better than to lust after.

"And you aren't," she waved a hand vaguely, "hoping to land a rich connected husband in the process?"

Chastity was glad she hadn't been drinking her tea at the moment, she would have spit. "Is that what Viktor said?" Hurt and anger flooded her.

"No, I'm just checking. It's my job to know the motivation before picking the angle," she said. "I can spin anything, but it's frustrating to spin a story one way and have the person switch sides after I've done all the good work."

Chastity wasn't sure she completely understood but she was starting to believe Sara wasn't here to judge, that was a relief.

A knock at the front door stopped any further questioning and Chastity hurried to answer it, recognizing the firm sound of Viktor's fist.

"Sara's already here," he said as way of greeting as he stepped inside adding to the hurt churning in her.

"Yeah, but I am not sure I understand why," she lied, but she wanted to hear what Viktor was hoping to gain from Sara's PR abilities.

"She's the best at this sort of thing."

"Containing scandals? Is that what we are to you?" she whispered, unable to keep the hurt out of her voice.

Viktor looked at her and she couldn't tell what was going on in his mind, but she would have given anything to. He opened his mouth to speak but Sara's voice from the living room stopped him.

"I just got a message from your father, he wants in on this. Can I set up a conference call?"

"No," Viktor snarled and walked past Chastity into the living room.

Chastity was slow to follow. She closed the front door carefully and went to the kitchen where she started making Viktor a cup of tea. She could hear the murmur of their voices in the other room, and she was thankful for a minute to herself. Her cell was on the counter and she picked it up, hands shaking. She opened her social media knowing she was going to see something she wasn't going to like. Her surprised face next to Viktor's snarling one was the first thing to greet her. The news was definitely out, and the comments beneath made her stomach hurt. Most comments debated whether or not Chastity had tricked and trapped the wealthy vampire into a relationship while others called her a liar outright, because human vampire pairings were extremely rare. There were comments about how Viktor should demand a paternity test, and so many that bemoaned the potential loss of such an eligible bachelor.

Everything pointed to one thing. This was a scandal, and she looked like the bad guy.

An email popped up and she clicked it, hoping it would distract her from the hole she was spiraling down. It was from the gallery downtown where she sold so much art. Bernard was informing her that due to recent news he'd be taking her paintings down because he didn't want to be seen as taking any side.

The unseen, unintended, and very unwelcome chaos of the goddess was really heaping it on today.

"Chastity, are you okay?" Viktor asked from the doorway.

"Oh, um, yeah. Here, I made you some tea." She handed him a cup of hot water and realized she'd forgotten the tea bag. She quickly grabbed one and dropped it in then went around him and out to the living room where Sara sat looking like a model, sipping tea.

"I need to get out from under this as soon as possible. What do we need to do?" Chastity asked. She couldn't let this ruin her livelihood and she didn't want it to ruin Viktor's life.

"I think the best solution is to go all out with the truth. Let the world know that this is a goddess gifted child and the clinic aided in the goddess's desire. That you two were unwilling participants but that you are dealing with it as adults the best as can be expected. That neither of you had any intention of making a political statement. This will all prove that Viktor wasn't tricked or coerced and certainly hasn't been trapped or tamed," she added with a wink and a laugh that Chastity didn't appreciate.

"It would probably be best for Viktor to be seen out with his usual bikini babes and you should find a different partner for Lamaze."

"N—" Viktor started.

"Of course," Chastity said, interrupting Viktor's dissent. "That sounds great, very smart."

"Chastity," Viktor growled.

"Viktor, you should probably spend as little time here as possible, and a parenting plan should be made public too. It would be good to let the vipers waiting for contention to have nothing to guess about," Sara said matter of factly.

"Sure, that makes perfect sense," Chastity said, her face frozen in a sort of grimace smile. It was taking everything she had to hold back the tears that were threatening to fall, and Viktor glaring at her didn't help.

"Okay, I'll set up a date for Viktor tonight and make sure the paparazzi know. Chastity, be ready to send out a statement on socials about everything. I'll email it to you. Johnson is offering to pay me for all of this. He must have figured you'd call me in, Viktor, but I'd rather take his money to be honest. So feel free to use me as much as you need to help with postings and such," she said brightly to both of them then stood.

She said goodbye quickly and was gone like the whirlwind she was.

"Chastity, I don't think—"

"I don't think you should be here," she interrupted. "It's bad press. I wouldn't want to ruin your reputation," she snapped and stood with as much dignity as she could and walked out of the room. She made it to her bed before the tears started to fall and when she heard the front door close behind Viktor, she curled into a ball and sobbed for everything she'd foolishly let herself believe she could have had with him.

Viktor left in a daze. That hadn't gone the way he'd expected. Chastity was so willing to go along with the spin Sara came up with, but why?

Sara startled him with a greeting as he approached his van. She was leaned next to the driver's door smoking a cigarette.

"Thanks for coming on such short notice," Viktor said.

"Your father pays well," she said with a shrug. "He called right after you."

"There's not a problem he can't throw money at, is there?"

She shrugged, "Maybe, maybe not. Hey, can I ask you something?" She paused, but not long enough for him to actually answer. "Do you have feelings for her?"

The question stabbed him in the heart because yeah, he did, and he had thought maybe she did too. But the way she'd responded in there, how quickly she'd agreed to everything. He wasn't so sure anymore and he couldn't help thinking it was probably for the best anyway.

"She's carrying my child, I care for them both."

Sara grunted. "Yeah, my brother said you're definitely falling in love with her, and I think he's right. Let me give you a little advice. Fuck her out of your system, don't fuck *her*, but fuck your usual beach babes and remember who you are. Johnson Paulie's playboy son and a great surf instructor. Stick with what you know, you aren't the relationship and white picket fence type. Shit, she has a literal white picket fence. She is not your style and neither is her life. Don't get caught up on the pheromones of her pregnancy, Viktor. You'd only end up hurting the poor thing and I think she's actually pretty cool for a human." Sara kissed his cheek and walked to her sleek black convertible.

Viktor stood staring at Chastity's house while Sara's words ran through his mind and he knew she was right. Chastity deserved so much more than what he could give her.

CHAPTER TWENTY-FIVE

Chastity showered when she was out of tears and dressed for a day at home, wallowing. She made herself breakfast and then, when she was feeling a little more brave, she opened her email. There was a message from Sara as she'd expected. It outlined the statement she was supposed to make on social media and even made some suggestions about what kind of photos she should add to the postings.

Anger bubbled up inside her and she slammed her laptop closed, picked up her phone and called a lawyer her father knew. Why was she going along with anything that involved Johnson Paulie?

By that afternoon she was back home with two copies of a parenting plan. It was one that made sense for the child, protected it from its grandfather, and was fair to both Viktor and herself. It wasn't ideal, of course. None of this was, but it was their reality and she needed to accept that. She sent a text to Viktor letting him know that she had a parenting agreement for him to sign. She didn't give him the option to contest, she didn't say it was for him to consider or look over. She said it was for him to sign. No matter how she told herself not to be, she was hurt, and she was mad that he hadn't defended her, hadn't fought for the blooming relationship they had.

He didn't respond but the little *read* sign came up.

Viktor wanted to scream when he saw Chastity's message. On top of what was in front of him, he was about to lose his shit. His father was standing in his shop with a sneer of disgust on his face as he looked around. The man had never set foot in Viktor's shop and for the first couple of years, that had bothered Viktor. It hadn't for a long time.

"I can't believe this is it. How do you make enough to survive?"

"Why are you here?" Viktor demanded, ignoring the insult.

"I am here to make sure you go through with the date set up. Sara found a girl happy for the chance to go out with you, and you need to make it look good. Have you gotten the human to sign the agreement yet?"

"No," Viktor grunted between clenched teeth, no use telling his father yet again that Chastity wouldn't be signing anything coming from him.

"Well, hurry it up. What is her deal, does she want more money? I was more than generous."

"I'll be signing an agreement with her tomorrow," Viktor said, *just not the one his father wanted.*

"Wonderful, now let's talk about this date. Don't get attached to the woman. I told Sara to have a different date ready for you tomorrow. We'll get pictures of you out with a different woman every night for the next week or so, make sure the press knows you haven't changed your ways due to this little fiasco. If you could manage to let the press get a walk of shame picture that would be even better. Fuck, I'd even go for a public sex scandal at this point. The wilder the better, I can easily spin my disappointment into votes."

Viktor blocked out the rest of his father's speech as his mind fired with denial. He couldn't do this; what would Chastity think of him? He didn't want to spend time with random women, he wanted to spend it with her. He had to fix this. He had to stop doing what his father wanted. Even this surf shop, this life he lived here, he knew that in a way it fed into the image of Johnson Paulie: *Just like every man, has a son who is worthless, but he still supports him.* He spun it all into votes, he didn't care about anything else.

"Fuck," Viktor snarled. The only time he'd actually done something against his father's interests was taking his sperm to the clinic. And the goddess had used that one true act of rebellion to give him a chance at the life he really wanted. Maybe She worked in chaotic mysterious ways, but did that make Her wrong? The white picket fence lifestyle could be for him, Sara was wrong. "I have to go," Viktor said, rushing past his father who was looking at him with shock.

"Your date is on her way, where the hell do you think you're going?"

"I need to fix the shit mess you made," Viktor snapped.

"Viktor," Johnson's harsh tone stopped Viktor at the door. "You will listen to me now, boy. *I* am fixing the shit mess *you* made. The only way this situation works is if you follow the direction I have outlined. The vampire community will never accept her, you can't be with her, not really, you know that right?"

Viktor turned and faced his father, allowing all of his childhood pain and adult disappointment for the man shine in his eyes. "I don't give a fuck about your rich politician vampires and their outdated ideas of what we should do. I am going to be with whoever the fuck I want, and that includes a human who is pregnant with my child."

Viktor left his father gaping and speechless. He'd never been so blunt with the man and it felt good.

. . .

Chastity was sipping tea with her father when Viktor knocked at her door. She hadn't expected him to show up, she was planning to drop the papers off to him, maybe hire a courier so she wouldn't have to actually see him.

"Do you want me to get rid of him?" her father asked when she just sat there, stiff.

She was tempted to say yes but knew it was probably best if she got Viktor to sign the papers right now. In fact, that had to be why he was here. He was just as anxious to get things settled as she was. She told herself that was a good thing, definitely for the best.

So why was her heart beating so fast and why were tears stinging her eyes?

She grabbed both copies of the parenting plan, already with her signature on them, and a pen. When she opened the door, the intense and agonized look on Viktor's face nearly stopped her but she was determined. "Here, sign both. One copy is for you, and one is for my lawyer."

"I will sign anything you want, but please, Chastity, please give me a chance," he begged.

"I didn't take your parental rights away," she said, confused. Did he think she was trying to completely cut him out?

He shook his head and stepped forward. She didn't move but kept the papers between them like a shield.

"I saw you. Two years ago I saw you on my beach in a bronze bikini with a sketch book. I saw that fucking adorable birth mark on your inner thigh and for the first time since I was a teenager my fangs popped out without my consent. I had to run inside and masturbate just to get them down and when I went back out to find you, you were already gone."

"And I think that's my sign to leave," her father said awkwardly and hurried from the kitchen.

Viktor didn't take his eyes off her as she said a hurried goodbye to her father. Once the man was gone, Viktor shut the front door and continued his story.

"I have fantasized about that birthmark every day since. I have scoured the beach for a dark blonde in a bronze bikini because I knew my life would never be complete until I knew what she tasted like. When I saw it again and you were spread out on an exam table carrying my child, I reacted just as dramatically but this time I knew who you were and it was like a dream come true wrapped in the most complicated mess the goddess could come up with. And then that night when you dropped your phone in the closet," he groaned and stepped closer. "I'm not ashamed to tell you I nearly came in my pants like a virgin."

He crowded her against the wall and she was on fire. His scent surrounded her and she sucked in deep breaths of it. She'd been afraid she'd never be this close to that delicious scent ever again. Every word he spoke was like a lick right to her core and she wanted to whine with the need she had for him. His eyes were dark and his fangs were protruding enough to slightly skew his words now. Knowing that it was desire for her that had them out made her want to grab him and demand that he show her exactly what those things could do.

"Chastity, I don't just want to be the father to this child. I want to be your partner in every way. I want to pick you up and take you to the bedroom and not let you out for days. I want to sustain myself on you and give you everything you could ever want or need. I want to spend every day waking in your arms and falling asleep with your scent surrounding me every night. Chastity, I have fallen in love with you." The last words were said with a crack in his voice.

Chastity gasped and reached up to drag his head down. She crushed her lips to his and pushed her tongue in deep, invading his mouth then dragged it against one sharp canine. The prick made them both groan and his hands went around her back, crushing her body to his. She felt his cock press against her belly, thick and hard.

"Bedroom," she demanded.

He lifted her easily and she wrapped her legs around his waist. They didn't break from the kiss as he walked to her bedroom.

"Is this safe?" he asked when they reached the bed.

"Pregnant women can have sex," she assured him.

"No, I mean, vampire sex. Usually it involves biting. Is it safe for me to bite you while you're pregnant?"

She flushed at his meaning, wanting that more than anything. "You're the vampire, you tell me."

Viktor groaned as she kissed along his jaw and nipped at his neck. She loved the taste of him, like sunshine and salt. His body was hard all over from surfing and she knew he'd be capable of many fun positions.

"Let me know if anything doesn't feel right," he said.

"Yes," she groaned as his head ducked to her neck and he sank his fangs into her.

Chastity had never been bitten before. She'd heard about it plenty and knew to expect a slight pinch and then just pleasure. What she hadn't known to expect was the straight pull it would have on her groin. With every gentle pull on her vein, her vaginal walls clenched, and her clit jolted. Wetness was practically pouring out of her by the time he pulled back and licked the wound and all she could do was cling to him and moan.

"Fuck, Chastity you taste amazing, sound amazing. You *are* amazing." He punctuated each compliment with a lick to the small wound on her neck.

"Thank you," she murmured, her head light and her body hot with need.

"I never want to taste anyone else's blood for the rest of my life." He laid her on the bed and started to undress her slowly. She was wearing a sundress so it wasn't long before she was laying naked and he stood back to look at her. His gaze devoured her from head to toe. When his eyes stopped on her slightly parted thighs, he groaned and reached out to stroke a finger over the strawberry birthmark.

"This is the first thing I ever noticed about you, but it isn't the best thing about you, Chastity, you are so amazing. Your art is brilliant, your bravery is to be admired, and the love I know you have for the people who are important to you is something I will work my entire life to deserve."

"Viktor," she gasped, wanting to tell him how she felt about him, but he stopped her with another deep kiss that had her tearing at his clothes, talk could wait, she needed him now. "Take these off or I am going to start ripping," she snarled.

He chuckled and pulled back, stripping his clothes off faster than she could have. He was over her before she had a chance to really appreciate his naked form, something else that could wait until other more pressing needs were satisfied. They were kissing again and this time she could feel his smooth naked skin hot against her. She ran her hands over his hard back down to his ass and squeezed. Damn, she'd wanted to do that for a while. He nipped at her lip as she dug her nails into the flesh there.

His knee prodded her legs apart and he kissed his way down her body, forcing her hands up onto his back. He paused to capture a nipple in his mouth and sucked gently on it.

"Ah, sensitive," she warned, and he grinned with her nipple between his lips before his tongue lashed it mercilessly. She grabbed his head and pulled him closer as her hips rolled up against his stomach. He licked at her nipple, being gentle but still pushing the boundary of pleasure to pain before moving to the other and attending to it the same way. She was soon moving against him in an embarrassingly frantic manner, rubbing her wet sex against him until he finally moved lower.

He kissed her belly a couple times, whispering things she couldn't quite hear but she assumed they weren't meant for her anyway. When he moved lower, she nearly screamed in indignation as he skipped passed her sex and instead pressed his open mouth to her birthmark.

She was half expecting a bite, but all he did was suck her skin into his mouth hard enough to leave a mark and then kiss it gently. "This is my third favorite spot on your body," he said, lifting slightly and meeting her gaze.

"Third?" she asked.

He nodded emphatically. "The first is your womb, carrying my child, and the second, I'm just guessing on this one, but it's that cunt that smells like heaven."

She laughed and he dove in then with licks and nips that had her gasping and grasping his hair. He drove her toward orgasm with expertise and when he pressed a finger to her opening it was all she could take. She arched her back and screamed at the ceiling as she rolled her hips against his mouth and came undone with the best orgasm she'd had in maybe ever.

When she was floating back to reality he gave one final loving lick to her weeping sex. She shivered and pulled his hair until he was face to face with her.

"That was even better than I thought it would be. Definitely my number two favorite place on your body. I plan to spend a lot of time there, I hope you don't mind," he said with a cocky grin.

"Don't mind at all. Now, I want to see that cock of yours," she said.

His eyes widened with surprise. "I can deny you nothing," he said and laid down beside her.

She missed the feel of him against her but the reward of sitting up and seeing his body laid out naked beside her was worth the loss. He was a beautiful specimen. He was vampire pale in the space his board shorts covered. His cock was a delicately darker shade that stood out stark against his paleness due to all the blood currently flowing into it and she licked her lips before bending forward and capturing the delicious treat in her mouth.

He groaned and touched her head reverently as she sucked and licked. The salty taste beading out of his tip made her moan. It wasn't different than a human man's.

"Fuck Chastity, I can't," he groaned. He grabbed her and lifted her above him, one hand held his cock up and the other helped guide her body down until he was just about to enter her.

"Vampires and humans can't pass disease, but I'm clean anyway," he assured her.

Chastity met his dark gaze and moaned, "Me too, the clinic tested me for everything and there's been no one since."

With a hiss of satisfaction he loosened his grip on her and she sunk down relishing the tight burn until she was full and gasping with the sensation. He was larger than she was used to, but in such a perfect way she never wanted anything else. When she was adjusted to his size, she started to move, hands on his chest as she rolled her hips.

"Look at me, Chastity," he demanded.

She opened her eyes, staring at him as she rocked on his cock. His hands were on her hips but he didn't try to control her, just groaned and moaned under her movements and she loved having the control over him, taking pleasure and giving it at the same time. It was a powerful feeling, watching his face wash over with pleasure as she moved, knowing she could stop and take it away or rush it forward, she could stretch it out, slow and torturously wonderful. She controlled his orgasm and she grinned down at him as his hands tightened on her hips when she started to move faster.

His lips curled back and his fangs glinted in the fading sunlight that streamed through the bedroom window. He was fierce and strong and all hers in that moment.

"Chastity," he groaned, one hand lifting up to squeeze her breast. "You're magnificent," he praised, and she felt beautiful.

The look in his eyes was more than desire and it melted her heart. He pinched her nipple which sent a new spike of pleasure through her and her movements became frantic with her second orgasm nearing. "Viktor please," she gasped, not sure what she was asking him for but knowing she didn't want the control anymore. He seemed to understand and moved one hand from her nipple to her clit and his other gripped her hip harder. He began to move her on his cock just the way she needed. He pinched her clit and she came, screaming out her pleasure while he roared under her, his hips stuttering up as his own orgasm exploded through him. His cock burst inside of her, filling her with a part of him that she already knew intimately.

As she lay collapsed on his chest, she couldn't hold back a giggle.

"Fuck, I don't think I've ever had a woman giggle after sex, was it that bad?" he asked as he stroked her hair and held her close.

"I was just thinking that this is the second time I've been shot full of your sperm but only the first time you've come inside me."

He laughed too, the deep sound rumbling his chest and shaking her body on top of his. "It is far from the last though, Chastity. I meant what I said. I want this, I want you. Can I be your white picket fence guy?"

Chastity lifted her head just enough to meet his gaze. She saw a vulnerability there that made her heart lurch.

"I fell in love with you too, Viktor. I really tried not to, but I did, and I want it all too. I want to be your white picket fence girl."

He moved fast, flipping them so she was beneath him and then he gave her a third orgasm leaving her boneless and happier than she'd ever been.

EPILOGUE: SIX MONTHS LATER

"Viktor I am going to rip your fucking head off if you don't get in here right now!"

Viktor smiled at his beautiful wife as he pushed back into the labor room with the ice chips she'd requested with just as much ferocity only five minutes earlier. "Sweet love, your father just parked, and my sister is in the waiting room, and I think they both heard that."

"Fuck them and fuck you, make it stop," she whined as the pain of the contraction ebbed. It had been a long labor so far and she was obviously exhausted. He didn't take it personally that she wanted to rip parts of his body off that she usually loved very much.

"Remember your breathing, we've been through this. Do you want to try sitting on the ball again?"

She nodded and he guided her to the yoga ball then rubbed her back as she swayed. He coached her breathing like Jenna had taught him as another contraction hit, followed very quickly by another and he knew it was time. His heart was beating wildly and aside from the moment two months before when she'd waddled down the beach toward him in a white dress, he had never felt so nervous and excited in his life. They still didn't know what exactly this little bundle was going to require, but it was going to have all the love and guidance it would need to make sure it grew up healthy and protected.

His sister poked her head in and smiled at him. "Dad just got here. He promised no photos and swears on my life, because you know I'm his favorite, that he only wants to be here as grandfather and not Johnson Paulie politician and grandfather to a famous hybrid vampire baby," she said making quotation marks with her fingers to indicate he'd said those exact words.

Viktor rolled his eyes but nodded. His father had made a lot of progress since Viktor had left him standing in his shop. He was starting to understand that this was Viktor's life and choice, not his. Viktor made sure that he also understood that he would only be allowed to be involved with the child under the parameters that he and Chastity set. Which was zero social media and zero political association. Though they had allowed him to post a wedding photo and would allow the announcement of the child, it would not be used as a political move, only as a social interest story about vampire and human relationships. There really was no way to get around the fact that this was a rare thing people would want to know about. The most important part would be that Viktor and Chastity controlled the aspects that were released to the public. Viktor had been reluctant to let the man into their life at all, but Chastity had encouraged it and slowly, together, they'd built a plan.

Johnson had agreed, though Viktor knew his father hadn't been happy about it, and doubted he'd heard the end of it. As husband and father, it would be Viktor's job to protect Chastity and the child from whatever came up in the future with his father's political aspirations though, and honestly he'd be happy to do it because it meant he had what he wanted. The white picket fence life with the woman of his dreams and a baby to love.

"Tell him it's almost time. He'll meet his grandchild soon."

"Good luck," Persia said and hurried out of the room as the doctor and more nurses rushed in.

"Viktor, I need to push," Chastity moaned and then things were happening faster than he could track.

"Here's your son," the nurse said as she handed Chastity a squealing naked mess of baby.

"A boy," she whispered, her tearful eyes meeting Viktor's. They had decided that this whole thing had been full of so many surprises, no reason to stop.

"My son," Viktor said reverently as he lightly touched the boy's wrinkled wet head. He had a soft blonde fuzz there and Chastity hoped he had hair like hers, but knew it was likely to all fall out and come back in as something different no matter what it looked like now.

"He has your butt," Viktor said as he studied the boy.

Chastity laughed and then regretted the harsh motion when she started to feel everything below the waist that ached and was no doubt damaged beyond recognition.

"No way, that dimple there on the left cheek, that's all you," she said.

He leaned down and kissed her. "You were amazing, and I will be forever grateful for this miracle."

"Thank the Moon Goddess, huh? Chaos and all, it turned out okay."

"More than okay," he agreed. "But the next one, let's do it the natural way," he said with a wink.

"I may never let you touch me again," she snarled.

"You'll change your mind soon enough," Martha called from the doorway. "Can I come in?"

"Yes! It's a boy, Martha, it's a perfect boy."

Martha hurried forward with her own young son strapped to

her chest. "They will be best friends," she said as she gazed down at the baby. "Did you check his eyes?"

Chastity shook her head. "I'm a little nervous, is that weird?" She met Viktor's understanding gaze.

"Not at all, and it doesn't matter. Whether he has vampire eyes or human ones, he's still perfect," Viktor assured her.

The baby was sleeping so it would have to wait anyway.

"I'll go make the announcement. Grandfathers and auntie are anxious to hear what we got," Martha said and left the room.

Persia hurried in then to coo and congratulate them. "What's his name?"

"Van Martin Paulie," Chastity announced proudly. It was a name that would serve him well.

"Welcome to the family, Van," Persia whispered with tears filling her eyes. "Fuck, now I want another one."

Chastity laughed and the movement woke Van up.

"Why don't you see if he'll eat," the nurse encouraged. "Then we can take him and do measurements."

With Viktor's help she sat up and adjusted Van. When the boy opened his eyes and looked up at her, everyone gasped.

"One blue and one red," Viktor gasped.

"I guess he really is a mix of us both," Chastity said and she was glad. It wasn't what she'd hoped for, planned for, and prayed for, when she started this whole process. It was so much better she knew, because not only did she have the child that she had always wanted, but she had a husband to hold her hand through the rest of her life.

"Dad is going to flip when he sees this," Persia laughed. "He'll be dying to put a picture of that on his campaign posters."

"Not a chance," Viktor said quietly as he helped guide his son to Chastity's breast.

A few hours later the families were gone, Van was dressed and wrapped up like a burrito, and Chastity was taking a shower.

Viktor held Van in his arms on the hospital bed and stared down at his perfect tiny features.

"I know you wanted to cause problems," he whispered into the night. "But thank you, Moon Goddess, thank you for giving me everything that I didn't know I wanted. I don't know what I did in a past life to deserve these two in my life, but I'll do everything I have to in order to deserve them for the rest of this one."

There was no answer, but he felt a warming in his body that he took as acknowledgement.

Felicity Stonecroft threw herbs into the fire and welcomed the answer of any spirit willing to talk. She wasn't surprised when the Moon Goddess appeared in the flames, She'd become a familiar entity in Felicity's life.

"And what kind of chaos are you hoping for now?" Felicity cackled.

A face and a number appeared in Felicity's mind.

"I am but a servant to your chaotic will," she said with a slick smile spreading across her face.

MEET THE AUTHOR

Courtney Davis is a romance author, teacher, and mother living in North Idaho. She writes across multiple romance genres creating stories that explore human and non-human interactions, loves, and more. She enjoys writing in any bit of spare time she can find and is never short on ideas for the next story, only on time to write them all from beginning to end.

OTHER TITLES FROM

5 PRINCE PUBLISHING

Soul Sacrifice *Courtney Davis*
Picking Pismo *Emi Hilton*
The Taste of Treachery *Emily Bybee*
Spring Showers *Sarah Dressler*
Secret Admirer Pact *Bernadette Marie*
The Publicity Stunt *Bernadette Marie*
A Trace of Romance *Ann Swann*
Descendants of Atlantis *Courtney Davis*
Holiday Rebound *Emily Bybee*
Rewriting Christmas *S.E. Reichert & Kerrie Flanagan*
Butterfly Kisses *Courtney Davis*
Leaving Cloverton *Emi Hilton*
Beach Rose Path *Barbara Matteson*
Aristotle's Wolves *Courtney Davis*